A FORG

M000279436

(KINGS AND SORCERERS—BOOK 4)

MORGAN RICE

"Valor is superior to number."

Flavius Vegetius Renatus
(4th century)

CHAPTER ONE

A cell door slammed, and Duncan slowly opened his eyes, wishing he hadn't. His head was throbbing, one eye was sealed shut, and he struggled to shake off the heavy sleep. A sharp pain shot through his good eye as he leaned back against cold, hard rock. Stone. He was lying on cold, damp stone. He tried to sit up, felt iron tugging at his wrists and ankles, rattling, and immediately, he realized: shackles. He was in a dungeon.

A prisoner.

Duncan opened his eyes wider as there came the distant sound of marching boots, echoing somewhere in the blackness. He tried to get his bearings. It was dark in here, stone walls dimly lit by torches flickering far away, by a small shaft of sunlight from a window too high up to see. The pale light filtered down, stark and lonely, as if from a world miles away. He heard a distant drip of water, a shuffle of boots, and he could just barely make out the contours of the cell. It was vast, its stone walls arched, with too many dark edges disappearing into blackness.

From his years in the capital, Duncan knew right away where he was: the royal dungeon. It was where they sent the kingdom's worst criminals, most powerful enemies, to rot away their days—or await their execution. Duncan had sent many men down here himself when he had served here, at the bequest of the King. It was a place, he knew too well, from which prisoners did not resurface.

Duncan tried to move, but his shackles wouldn't let him, cutting into his bruised and bleeding wrists and ankles. These, though, were the least of his ailments; his entire body ached and throbbed, in so much pain that he could hardly decipher where it hurt most. He felt as if he had been clubbed a thousand times, stampeded by an army of horses. It hurt to breathe, and he shook his head, trying to make it go away. It would not.

As he closed his eyes, licked his chapped lips, Duncan saw flashes. The ambush. Had it been yesterday? A week ago? He could no longer recall. He had been betrayed, surrounded, lured by promises of a false deal. He had trusted Tarnis, and Tarnis, too, had been killed, before his eyes.

Duncan remembered his men dropping their weapons at his command; remembered being restrained; and worst of all, he remembered his sons' murders.

He shook his head again and again as he cried out in anguish, trying fruitlessly to wipe the images from his mind. He sat with his head in his hands, his elbows on his knees, and moaned at the thought. How could he have been so stupid? Kavos had warned him, and he had not heeded the warning, being naively optimistic, thinking it would be different this time,

7

that the nobles could be trusted. And he had led his men right into a trap, right into a den of snakes.

Duncan hated himself for it, more than he could say. His only regret was that he was still alive, that he had not died back there with his sons, and with all the others he had let down.

The footsteps came louder, and Duncan looked up and squinted into the darkness. Slowly there emerged the silhouette of a man, blocking the shaft of sunlight, approaching until he stood but a few feet away. As the man's face took shape, Duncan recoiled with recognition. The man, easily distinguishable in his aristocratic dress, wore the same pompous look he'd had when petitioning Duncan for the kingship, when trying to betray his father. Enis. Tarnis's son.

Enis knelt before Duncan, a smug, victorious smile on his face, the long vertical scar on his ear noticeable as he stared back with his shifty, hollow eyes. Duncan felt a wave of revulsion, a burning desire for vengeance. He clenched his fists, wanting to lunge for the boy, to tear him apart with his own hands, this boy who had been responsible for the death of his sons, for his men's imprisonment. The shackles were all that was left in the world to keep him from killing him.

"The shame of iron," Enis remarked, smiling. "Here I kneel, but inches from you, and you are powerless to touch me."

Duncan glared back, wishing he could speak, yet too exhausted to form words. His throat was too dry, his lips too parched, and he needed to conserve his energy. He wondered how many days it had been since he'd had water, how long he'd been down here. This weasel, anyway, was not worth his speech.

Enis was down here for a reason; clearly he wanted something. Duncan had no false illusions: he knew that, no matter what this boy had to say, his execution was looming. Which was what he wanted, anyway. Now that his sons were dead, his men imprisoned, there was nothing left for him in this world, no other way to escape his guilt.

"I am curious," Enis said, in his slick voice. "How does it feel? How does it feel to have betrayed everyone you know and love, everyone who trusted you?"

Duncan felt his rage flare up. Unable to keep silent any longer, he somehow summoned the strength to speak.

"I betrayed no one," he managed to say, his voice gravelly and hoarse.

"Didn't you?" Enis retorted, clearly enjoying this. "They trusted you. You walked them right into ambush, surrender. You stripped the last thing they had left: their pride and honor."

Duncan fumed with each breath.

"No," he finally replied, after a long and heavy silence. "You are the one who stripped that away. I trusted your father, and he trusted you."

8

"Trust," Enis laughed. "What a naïve concept. Would you really stake men's lives in trust?"

He laughed again, as Duncan fumed.

"Leaders don't trust," he continued. "Leaders doubt. That is their job, to be skeptical on behalf of all their men. Commanders protect men from battle—but leaders must protect men from deception. You are no leader. You failed them all."

Duncan took a deep breath. A part of him could not help but feel that Enis was right, as much as he hated to admit it. He had failed his men, and it was the worst feeling of his life.

"Is that why you have come here?" Duncan finally replied. "To gloat over your deception?"

The boy smiled, an ugly, evil smile.

"You are my subject now," he replied. "I am your new King. I can go anywhere, anytime I wish, for any reason, or for no reason at all. Maybe I just like to look at you, lying here in the dungeon, as broken as you are."

Duncan breathed, each breath hurting, barely able to control his rage. He wanted to hurt this man more than anyone he'd ever met.

"Tell me," Duncan said, wanting to hurt him. "How did it feel to murder your father?"

Enis's expression hardened.

"Not half as good as it will feel when I watch you die in the gallows," he replied.

"Then do it now," Duncan said, meaning it.

Enis smiled, though, and shook his head.

"It won't be that easy for you," he replied. "I will watch you suffer first. I want you to first see what will become of your beloved country. Your sons are dead. Your commanders are dead. Anvin and Durge and all your men at the Southern Gate are dead. Millions of Pandesians have invaded our nation."

Duncan's heart sank at the boy's words. Part of him wondered if this was a trick, yet he sensed it was all true. He felt himself sinking lower into the earth with each proclamation.

"All of your men are imprisoned, and Ur is being bombarded by sea. So you see, you have failed miserably. Escalon is far worse off than it was before, and you have no one to blame but yourself."

Duncan shook with rage.

"And how long," Duncan asked, "until the great oppressor turns on you? Do you really think you shall be exempt, that you will escape Pandesia's wrath? That they will allow you to be King? To rule as your father once did?"

Enis smiled wide, resolute.

"I *know* that they will," he said.

9

He leaned in close, so close that Duncan could smell his bad breath.

"You see, I've made them a deal. A very special deal to ensure my power, a deal that was too much for them to turn down."

Duncan dared not ask what it was, yet Enis smiled wide and leaned in.

"Your daughter," he whispered.

Duncan's eyes widened.

"Did you really think you could hide her whereabouts from me?" Enis pressed. "As we speak, Pandesians are closing in on her. And that gift will cement my place in power."

Duncan's shackles rattled, the noise echoing throughout the dungeon, as he struggled with all his might to break free and attack, filled with a despair beyond what he could bear.

"Why have you come?" Duncan asked, feeling much older, his voice broken. "What is it that you want from me?"

Enis grinned. He fell silent for a long time, then finally sighed.

"I believe that my father wanted something of you," he said slowly. "He would not have summoned you, would not have brokered that deal, unless he did. He offered you a great victory with the Pandesians—and in return, he would have requested something. What? What was it? What secret was he hiding?"

Duncan stared back, resolute, no longer caring.

"Your father did wish for something," he said, rubbing it in. "Something honorable and sacred. Something he could trust with only me. Not his own son. Now I know why."

Enis sneered, flushed red.

"If my men died for anything," Duncan continued, "it was for this sake of honor and trust—one that I would never break. Which is why you shall never know."

Enis darkened, and Duncan was pleased to see him enraged.

"Would you still guard the secrets of my dead father, the man who betrayed you and all your men?"

"*You* betrayed me," Duncan corrected, "not he. He was a good man who once made a mistake. You, on the other hand, are nothing. You are but a shadow of your father."

Enis scowled. He slowly rose to his full height, leaned over, and spit beside Duncan.

"You will tell me what he wanted," he insisted. "What—or who—he was trying to hide. If you do, I might just be merciful and free you. If not, I will not only escort you to the gallows myself, but I will see to it that you die the most gruesome death imaginable. The choice is yours, and there is no turning back. Think hard, Duncan."

Enis turned to leave, but Duncan called out.

"You can have my answer now if you wish," Duncan replied.

Enis turned, a satisfied look on his face.

"I choose death," he replied, and for the first time, managed to smile. "After all, death is nothing next to honor."

CHAPTER TWO

Dierdre, wiping sweat from her forehead as she labored away in the forge, suddenly sat up, jolted by a thunderous noise. It was a distinct noise, one that set her on edge, a noise that rose above the din of all the hammers striking anvils. All the men and women around her stopped, too, laid down their unfinished weapons, and looked out, puzzled.

It came again, sounding like thunder rolling on the wind, sounding as if the very fabric of the earth were being torn apart.

Then again.

Finally, Dierdre realized: iron bells. They were tolling, striking terror in her heart as they slammed again and again, echoing throughout the city. They were bells of warning, of danger. Bells of war.

All at once the people of Ur jumped up from their tables and rushed out of the forge, all eager to see. Dierdre was first among them, joined by her girls, joined by Marco and his friends, and they all burst outside and entered streets flooded with concerned citizens, all flocking toward the canals to get a better view. Dierdre searched everywhere, expecting, with those bells, to see her city overrun with ships, with soldiers. Yet she did not.

Puzzled, she headed toward the massive watchtowers perched at the edge of the Sorrow, wanting to get a better view.

"Dierdre!"

She turned to see her father and his men, all running for the watchtowers, too, all eager to get an open view of the sea. All four towers rang frantically, something that never happened, as if death itself were approaching the city.

Dierdre fell in beside her father as they ran, turning down streets and ascending a set of stone steps until they finally reached the top of the city wall, at the edge of the sea. She stopped there, beside him, stunned at the sight before her.

It was like her worst nightmare come to life, a sight she wished she'd never seen in her lifetime: the entire sea, all the way to the horizon, was filled with black. The black ships of Pandesia, so close together that they covered the water, seemed to cover the entire world. Worst of all, they all bore down in a singular force right for her city.

Dierdre stood frozen, staring at the coming death. There was no way they could defend against a fleet that size, not with their meager chains, and not with their swords. When the first ships reached the canals, they could bottleneck them, maybe, delay them. They could perhaps kill hundreds or even thousands of soldiers.

But not the millions she saw before her.

Dierdre felt her heart ripping in two as she turned and looked to her father, his soldiers, and saw the same silent panic in their faces. Her father put on a brave face before his men, but she knew him. She could see the fatalism in his eyes, see the light fade from them. All of them, clearly, were staring at their deaths, at the end of their great and ancient city.

Beside her, Marco and his friends looked out with terror, but also with resolve, none of them, to their credit, turning and running away. She searched the sea of faces for Alec, but she was puzzled not to find him anywhere. She wondered where he could have gone. Surely he would not have fled?

Dierdre stood her ground and tightened her grip on her sword. She knew death was coming for them—she just had not expected it so soon. She was done, though, running from anyone.

Her father turned to her and grabbed her shoulders with urgency.

"You must leave the city," he demanded.

Dierdre saw the fatherly love in his eyes, and it touched her.

"My men will escort you," he added. "They can get you far from here. Go now! And remember me."

Dierdre wiped away a tear as she saw her father looking down at her with so much love. She shook her head and brushed his hands off of her.

"No, Father," she said. "This is my city, and I will die by your—"

Before she could finish her words, a horrific explosion cut through the air. At first she was confused, thinking it was another bell, but then she realized—cannon fire. Not just one cannon, but hundreds of them.

The shock waves alone knocked Dierdre off balance, cutting through the fabric of the atmosphere with such force, she felt as if her ears were split in two. Then came the high-pitched whistle of cannonballs, and as she looked out to sea, she felt a wave of panic as she saw hundreds of massive cannonballs, like iron cauldrons in the sky, arching high and heading right for her beloved city.

There followed another sound, worse than the last: the sound of iron crushing stone. The very air rumbled as there came one explosion after another. Dierdre stumbled and fell as all around her the great buildings of Ur, architectural masterpieces, monuments that had lasted thousands of years, were destroyed. These stone buildings, ten feet thick, churches, watchtowers, fortifications, battlements—all, to her horror, were smashed to bits by cannonballs. They crumbled before her eyes.

There came an avalanche of rubble as one building after another toppled to the ground.

It was sickening to watch. As Dierdre rolled on the ground, she saw a hundred-foot stone tower begin to fall on its side. She was helpless to do anything but watch as she saw hundreds of people beneath it look up and shriek in terror as the wall of stone crushed them.

There followed another explosion.

And another.

And another.

All around her more and more buildings exploded and fell, thousands of people instantly crushed in massive plumes of dust and debris. Boulders rolled throughout the city like pebbles while buildings fell into each other, crumbling as they landed on the ground. And still the cannonballs kept coming, ripping through one precious building after the other, turning this once majestic city into a mound of rubble.

Dierdre finally regained her feet. She looked about, dazed, ears ringing, and between clouds of dust saw streets filled with corpses, pools of blood, as if the whole city had been wiped out in an instant. She looked to the seas and saw the thousands more ships waiting to attack, and she realized that all their planning had been a joke. Ur was already destroyed, and the ships had not even touched shore. What good would all those weapons, all those chains and spikes, do now?

Dierdre heard moaning and looked over to see one of her father's brave men, a man she had once loved dearly, lying dead but feet away from her, crushed by a pile of rubble that should have landed on her, had she not stumbled and fell. She went to go to help him—when the air suddenly shook with the roar of another round of cannonballs.

And another.

Whistling followed, then more explosions, more buildings falling. Rubble piled higher, and more people died, as she was knocked to her feet yet again, a wall of stone collapsing beside her and narrowly missing her.

There came a lull in the firing, and Dierdre stood. A wall of rubble now blocked her view of the sea, yet she sensed the Pandesians were close now, at the beach, which was why the firing had stopped. Huge clouds of dust hung in the air, and in the eerie silence, there came nothing but the moans of the dead all around her. She looked over to see Marco beside her, crying out in distress as he tried to yank free the body of one of his friends. Dierdre looked down and saw the boy was already dead, crushed beneath the wall of what was once a temple.

She turned, remembering her girls, and was devastated to see several of them also crushed to death. But three of them survived, trying, fruitlessly, to save the others.

There came the shout of the Pandesians, on foot, on the beach, charging for Ur. Dierdre thought of her father's offer, and knew that his men could still whisk her away from here. She knew that remaining here would mean her death—yet that was what she wanted. She would not run.

Beside her, her father, a gash across his forehead, rose up from the rubble, drew his sword, and fearlessly led his men in a charge for the pile of rubble. He was, she realized proudly, rushing to meet the enemy. It

14

would be a battle on foot now, and hundreds of men rallied behind him, all rushing forward with such fearlessness that it filled her with pride.

She followed, drawing her sword and climbing the huge boulders before her, ready to do battle by his side. As she scrambled to the top, she stopped, stunned at the sight before her: thousands of Pandesian soldiers, in their yellow and blue armor, filled the beach, charging for the mound of rubble. These men were well trained, well armed, and rested—unlike her father's men, who numbered but a few hundred, with crude weapons and all already wounded.

It would, she knew, be a slaughter.

And yet her father didn't turn back. She was never more proud of him than she was in that moment. There he stood, so proud, his men gathered around him, all ready to rush down to meet the enemy, even though it would mean a sure death. It was, for her, the very embodiment of valor.

As he stood there, before he descended, he turned and looked at Dierdre with a look of such love. There was a goodbye in his eyes, as if he knew he would never see her again. Dierdre was confused—her sword was in hand, and she was preparing to charge with him. Why would he be saying goodbye to her now?

She suddenly felt strong hands grab her from behind, felt herself yanked backwards, and she turned to see two of her father's trusted commanders grabbing her. A group of his men also grabbed her three remaining girls, and Marco and his friends. She bucked and protested, but it was no use.

"Let me go!" she screamed.

They ignored her protests as they dragged her away, clearly at her father's command. She caught one last look at her father before he led his men down the other side of the rubble in a great battle cry.

"Father!" she cried.

She felt torn apart. Just as she was truly admiring the father she loved again, he was being taken from her. She wanted to be with him desperately. But he was already gone.

Dierdre found herself thrown on a small boat, and immediately the men began rowing down the canal, away from the sea. The boat turned again and again, cutting through the canals, heading toward a secret side opening in one of the walls. Before them loomed a low stone arch, and Dierdre recognized immediately where they were going: the underground river. It was a raging current on the other side of that wall, and it would lead them far away from the city. She would emerge somewhere many miles away from here, safe and sound in the countryside.

All her girls turned to look to her, as if wondering what they should do. Dierdre came to an immediate decision. She pretended to acquiesce to the plan, so that they would all go. She wanted them all to escape, to be free from this place.

Dierdre waited until the last moment, and just before they entered, she leapt from the boat, landing in the waters of the canal. Marco, to her surprise, noticed her and jumped, too. That left only the two of them floating in the canal.

"Dierdre!" shouted her father's men.

They turned to grab her—but it was too late. She had timed it perfectly, and they were already caught up in the gushing currents, sweeping their boat away.

Dierdre and Marco turned and swam quickly for an abandoned boat, boarding it. They sat there, dripping wet, and stared at each other, each breathing hard, exhausted.

Dierdre turned and looked back to where they had come from, to the heart of Ur, where she had left her father's side. It was there she would go, there and nowhere else, even if it meant her death.

CHAPTER THREE

Merk stood at the entrance to the hidden chamber, on the top floor of the Tower of Ur, Pult, the traitor, lying dead at his feet, and he stared into the shining light. The door ajar, he could not believe what he saw.

Here it was, the sacred chamber, on the most protected floor, the one and only room designed to hold and guard the Sword of Fire. Its door was carved with the insignia of the sword and its stone walls, too, had the sword's insignia carved into them. It was this room, and this room alone, that the traitor had wanted, to steal the most sacred relic of the kingdom. If Merk had not caught him and killed him, who knows where the Sword would be now?

As Merk stared into the room, its stone walls smooth, shaped in a circle, as he stared into the shining light, he began to see that there, in the center, sat a golden platform, a flaming torch beneath it, a steel cradle above, clearly designed to hold the Sword. And yet, as he stared, he could not understand what he saw.

The cradle was empty.

He blinked, trying to understand. Had the thief stolen the Sword already? No, the man was dead at his feet. That could only mean one thing.

This tower, the sacred Tower of Ur, was a decoy. All of it—the room, the tower—all a decoy. The Sword of Fire did not reside here. It had never resided here.

If not, then where could it be?

Merk stood there, horrified, too frozen to move. He thought back to all the legends surrounding the Sword of Fire. He recalled mention of the two towers, the Tower of Ur in the northwest corner of the kingdom, and the Tower of Kos in the southeast, each placed on opposite ends of the kingdom, each counterbalancing each other. He knew that only one of them held the Sword. And yet Merk had always assumed that *this* tower, the Tower of Ur, was the one. Everyone in the kingdom assumed that; everyone pilgrimaged to this tower alone, and the legends themselves always hinted at Ur as being the one. After all, Ur was on the mainland, close to the capital, near a great and ancient city—while Kos was at the end of the Devil's Finger, a remote location with no significance and not close to anything.

It had to be in Kos.

Merk stood there, in shock, and it slowly dawned on him: he was the only one in the kingdom who knew the true location of the Sword. Merk did not know what secrets, what treasures, this Tower of Ur held, if any, but he knew for certain that it did not hold the Sword of Fire. He felt deflated. He had learned what he was not meant to learn: that he and all the other soldiers here were guarding nothing. It was knowledge that the Watchers were not supposed to have—for, of course, it would demoralize them. After all, who would want to guard an empty tower?

Now that Merk knew the truth, he felt a burning desire to flee this place, to head to Kos, and to protect the Sword. After all, why remain here and guard empty walls?

Merk was a simple man, and he hated riddles above all else, and this all gave him a huge headache, raising more questions for him than answers. Who else might know this? Merk wondered. The Watchers? Surely some of them must know. If they knew, how could they possibly have the discipline to spend all their days guarding a decoy? Was that all part of their practice? Of their sacred duty?

Now that he knew, what should he do? Certainly he could not tell the others. That could demoralize them. They might not even believe him, thinking he had stolen the Sword.

And what should he do with this dead body, this traitor? And if this traitor was trying to steal the Sword, was anyone else? Had he been acting alone? Why would he want to steal it anyway? Where would he take it?

As he stood there trying to figure it all out, suddenly, his hair stood on end as bells tolled so loud, just feet from his head, sounding as if they were in this very room. They were so immediate, so urgent, he could not understand where they were coming from—until he realized the bell tower, atop the roof, was but feet from his head. The room shook with their incessant tolling, and he couldn't think straight. After all, their urgency implied that they were bells of war.

A commotion suddenly arose from all corners of the tower. Merk could hear the distant ruckus, as if everyone inside were rallying. He had to know what was going on; he could come back to this dilemma later.

Merk dragged the body out of the way, slammed the door closed, and ran from the room. He rushed into the hall and saw dozens of warriors rushing up the stairs, all with swords in hand. At first he wondered if they were coming for him, but then he looked up, saw more men rushing up the stairs, and realized they were all heading to the roof.

Merk joined them, rushing up the stairs, bursting onto the roof amidst the deafening tolling of the bells. He rushed to the edge of the tower and looked out—and was stunned when he did. His heart fell as he saw in the distance the Sea of Sorrow, covered in black, a million ships converging on the city of Ur in the distance. The fleet did not seem to be heading to the Tower of Ur, though, which sat a good day's ride north of the city, so with no immediate danger, Merk wondered why these bells were tolling so urgently.

18

Then he saw the warriors turning in the opposite direction. He turned, too, and saw it: there, emerging from the woods, was a band of trolls. These were followed by more trolls.

And more.

There came a loud rustling, followed by a roar, and suddenly, hundreds of trolls burst forth from the forest, shrieking, charging, halberds held high, blood in their eyes. Their leader was out front, the troll known as Vesuvius, a grotesque beast carrying two halberds, his face covered in blood. They were all converging on the tower.

Merk realized right away that this was no ordinary troll attack. It seemed as if the entire nation of Marda had broken through. How had they made it past the Flames? he wondered. They had all clearly come here looking for the Sword, wanting to lower the Flames. Ironic, Merk thought, given that the Sword was not here.

The tower, Merk realized, could not withstand such an onslaught. It was finished.

Merk felt a sense of dread, steeling himself for the final fight of his life, as he was encircled. All around him warriors clenched their swords, looking down in panic.

"MEN!" Vicor, Merk's commander, shrieked. "TAKE UP POSITIONS!"

The warriors took up positions all along the battlements and Merk immediately joined them, rushing to the edge, grabbing a bow and quiver, as did the others around him, taking aim and firing.

Merk was pleased to watch one of his arrows impale a troll in the chest; yet, to his surprise, the beast continued to run, even with an arrow protruding through his back. Merk fired at him again, sending an arrow into the troll's neck—and still, to his shock, it continued to run. He fired a third time, hitting the troll in the head, and this time the troll fell to the ground.

Merk fast realized that these trolls were no ordinary adversaries, and would not go down as easily as men. Their chances seemed more dire. Still, he fired again and again, dropping as many trolls as he could. Arrows rained down from all of his fellow soldiers, too, blackening the sky, sending trolls stumbling and falling, clogging the way for others

But too many broke through. They soon reached the thick tower walls, raised halberds, and slammed them against the golden doors, trying to knock them down. Merk could feel the vibrations underfoot, setting him on edge.

The clanging of metal ran through the air, as the nation of trolls slammed against the doors relentlessly. Somehow, Merk was relieved to see, the doors held. Even with hundreds of trolls smashing into it, the doors, as if by magic, did not even bend or even dent.

"BOULDERS!" Vicor yelled.

Merk saw the other soldiers rush over to a mound of boulders lined up along the edge, and he joined them as they all reached over and hoisted one. Together, he and ten others managed to lift it and push it up toward the top of the wall. Merk strained and groaned beneath the effort, hoisting it with all his might, then finally they all pushed it over with a great shout.

Merk leaned over with the others and watched as the boulder fell, whistling through the air.

The trolls below looked up—but too late. It crushed a group of them into the ground, flattening them, leaving a huge crater in the earth beside the tower wall. Merk helped the other soldiers as they hoisted boulders over the edge on all sides of the tower, killing hundreds of trolls, the earth shaking with the explosions.

Yet still they came, an endless stream of trolls, bursting forth from the wood. Merk saw they were out of boulders; they were out of arrows, too, and the trolls showed no sign of slowing down.

Merk suddenly felt something whiz by his ear, and he turned to see a spear fly by. He looked down, baffled, and saw the trolls taking up spears, hurling them up at the battlements. He was amazed; he had no idea they had the strength to throw that far.

Vesuvius led them, raising a golden spear and throwing it high, straight up, and Merk watched in shock as the spear reached the top of the tower and just missed him as he ducked. He heard a groan, and turned to see that his fellow soldiers were not so lucky. Several of them lay on their backs, pierced by the spears, blood pouring from their mouths.

Even more disturbing, there came a rumbling noise, and suddenly from out of the wood there rolled forth an iron battering ram, carried on a cart with wooden wheels. The crowd of trolls parted way as the ram was rolled forward, led by Vesuvius, right for the door.

"SPEARS!" cried Vicor.

Merk ran over with the others to the mound of spears, knowing as he grabbed one that this was their last line of defense. He had thought they would save these until the trolls breached the tower, leaving them a last line of defense, but apparently, times were desperate. He grabbed one, took aim, and hurled it down, aiming for Vesuvius.

But Vesuvius was faster than he looked and he dodged at the last moment. Merk's spear instead hit another troll in the thigh, dropping him, slowing the approach of the battering ram. His fellow soldiers threw them and spears hailed down, killing the trolls pushing the battering ram and stopping its progress.

Yet as soon as the trolls fell, a hundred more appeared from the wood, replacing them. Soon the ram rolled forward again. There were just too many of them—and they were all dispensable. This was not the way that humans fought. This was a nation of monsters.

20

Merk reached out for another spear to throw, and he was dismayed to find none left. At the same time, the battering ram reached the tower's doors, several trolls laying down planks of wood over the craters to form a bridge.

"FORWARD!" Vesuvius shouted far below, his voice deep and gravelly.

The group of trolls charged and shoved the ram forward. A moment later it smashed the doors with such force that Merk could feel the vibration all the way up here. The tremor ran through his ankles, hurting him down to the bone.

It came again, and again, and again, shaking the tower, causing him and the others to stumble. He landed on his hands and knees atop a body, a fellow Watcher, only to realize he was already dead.

Merk heard a whizzing noise, felt a wave of wind and heat, and as he looked up he could not comprehend what he saw: overhead flew a boulder of fire. Explosions rang out all around him as flaming boulders landed atop the tower. Merk squatted and looked over the edge to see dozens of catapults being fired from below, aimed at the roof of the tower. All around him, his men were dying.

Another flaming boulder landed near Merk, killing two Watchers beside him, men he had grown to like, and as the flames spread out, he could feel them near his own back. Merk looked about, saw nearly all the men dead around him, and he knew there was nothing more he could do up here, except wait to die.

Merk knew it was now or never. He was not going to go down like this, huddled atop the tower, awaiting death. He would go down bravely, fearlessly, facing the enemy with a dagger in hand, face to face, and kill as many of these creatures as he could.

Merk let out a great cry, reached for the rope affixed to the tower, and jumped over the edge. He slid down it at full speed, heading for the nation of trolls below, and ready to meet his destiny.

CHAPTER FOUR

Kyra blinked as she gazed up at the sky, the world in motion above her. It was the most beautiful sky she had ever seen, deep purple, with soft white clouds drifting overhead, the sky aglow with diffused sunlight. She felt herself moving, and she heard the gentle lapping of water all around her. She had never felt such a deep sense of peace.

On her back, Kyra looked over and was surprised to see she was floating in the midst of a vast sea, on a wooden raft, far from any shore. Huge, rolling waves gently lifted her raft up and down. She felt as if she were drifting to the horizon, to another world, another life. To a place of peace. For the first time in her life, she no longer worried about the world; she felt wrapped in the embrace of the universe, as if, finally, she could let down her guard and be taken care of, shielded from all harm.

Kyra sensed another presence on her boat, and she sat up and was startled to see a woman sitting there. The woman wore white robes, shrouded in light, with long golden hair and startling blue eyes. She was the most beautiful woman Kyra had ever seen.

Kyra felt a sense of shock as she felt certain that this was her mother.

"Kyra, my love," the woman said.

The woman smiled down at her, such a sweet smile that it restored Kyra's soul, and Kyra looked back and felt an even deeper sense of peace. The voice resonated through her, made her feel at peace in the world.

"Mother," she replied.

Her mother held out a hand, nearly translucent, and Kyra reached up and grasped it. The feel of her skin was electrifying, and as she held it, Kyra felt as though a part of her own soul were being restored.

"I've been watching you," she said. "And I am proud. More proud than you will ever know."

Kyra tried to focus, but as she felt the warmth of her mother's embrace, she felt as if she were leaving this world.

"Am I dying, Mother?"

Her mother looked back, her eyes aglow, and gripped her hand tighter.

"It is your time, Kyra," she said. "And yet, your courage has changed your destiny. Your courage—and my love."

Kyra blinked back, confused.

"Will we not be together now?"

Her mother smiled at her, and Kyra felt her mother slowly letting go, drifting away. Kyra felt a rush of fear as she knew her mother would leave, be gone forever. Kyra tried to hold onto her, but she withdrew her hand and instead placed her palm on Kyra's stomach. Kyra felt intense heat and love coursing through it, healing her. Slowly, she felt herself being restored.

22

"I will not let you die," her mother replied. "My love for you is stronger than fate."

Suddenly, her mother disappeared.

In her place stood a beautiful boy, staring back at her with glowing grey eyes, long, straight hair, mesmerizing her. She could feel the love in his gaze.

"I, too, will not let you die, Kyra," he echoed.

He leaned in, placed his palm on her stomach, the same place her mother's had been, and she felt an even more intense heat course through her body. She saw a white light and felt heat gushing through her, and as she felt herself coming back to life she could barely breathe.

"Who are you?" she asked, her voice barely above a whisper.

Drowning in the heat and the light, she could not help but close her eyes.

Who are you? echoed in her mind.

Kyra opened her eyes slowly, feeling an intense wave of peace, of calm. She looked all about, expecting to still be on the ocean, to see the water, the sky.

Instead, she heard the ubiquitous chirping of insects. She turned, confused, to find herself in the woods. She was lying in a clearing and she felt intense heat radiating in her stomach, the place where she had been stabbed, and she looked down to see a single hand there. It was a beautiful, pale hand, touching her stomach, as it had in her dream. Lightheaded, she looked up to see those beautiful grey eyes staring down at her, so intense, they seemed to be glowing.

Kyle.

He knelt at her side, one hand on her forehead, and as he touched her, Kyra slowly felt her wound being healed, slowly felt herself returning to this world, as if he were willing her back. Had she really visited with her mother? Had it been real? She felt as if she had been meant to die, and yet somehow, her destiny had been changed. It was as if her mother had intervened. And Kyle. Their love had brought her back. That, and, as her mother had said, her own courage.

Kyra licked her lips, too weak to sit up. She wanted to thank Kyle, but her throat was too parched and the words would not come out.

"Shh," he said, seeing her struggle, leaning forward and kissing her forehead.

"Did I die?" she finally managed to ask.

After a long silence he answered, his voice soft, yet powerful.

"You have come back," he said. "I would not let you go."

It was a strange feeling; looking into his eyes, she felt as if she had always known him. She reached out and grabbed his wrist, squeezing it, so grateful. There was so much she wanted to say to him. She wanted to ask him why he would risk his life for her; why he cared so much about her; why he would sacrifice to bring her back. She sensed he had, indeed, made a great sacrifice for her, a sacrifice that would somehow hurt him.

Most of all, she wanted him to know what she was feeling right now.

I love you, she wanted to say.

But the words would not come out. Instead, a wave of exhaustion overcame her, and as her eyes closed, she had no choice but to succumb. She felt herself falling deeper and deeper into sleep, the world racing by her, and she wondered if she were dying again. Had she only been brought back for a moment? Had she come back one last time just to say goodbye to Kyle?

And as a deep slumber finally overtook her, she could have sworn she heard a few last words before she drifted off for good:

"I love you, too."

CHAPTER FIVE

The baby dragon flew in agony, each flap of his wings an effort, struggling to stay in the air. He flew, as he had for hours, over the countryside of Escalon, feeling lost and alone in this cruel world he had been born into. There flashed through his mind images of his dying father, lying there, his great eyes closing, being jabbed to death by all those human soldiers. His father, whom he had never had a chance to know, except for that one moment of glorious battle; his father, who had died saving him.

The baby dragon felt his father's death as if it were his own, and with each flap of his wings, he felt more burdened by the guilt. If it were not for him, his father might be alive right now.

The dragon flew, torn with grief and remorse at the idea that he would never have a chance to know his father, to thank him for his selfless act of valor, for saving his life. A part of him no longer wanted to live either.

Another part, though, burned with rage, was desperate to kill those humans, to avenge his father and destroy the land below him. He did not know where he was, yet he sensed intuitively that he was oceans away from his homeland. Some instinct drove him to go back home; yet he did not know where home was.

The baby flew aimlessly, so lost in the world, breathing flames on treetops, on whatever he could find. Soon he ran out of fire, and soon after that, he found himself dipping lower and lower, with each flap of the wing. He tried to rise, but he found, in a panic, that he no longer had the strength. He tried to avoid a treetop, but his wings could no longer lift him, and he smashed right into it, smarting from all the old wounds that had not healed.

In agony, he bounced off it and continued flying, his elevation continually decreasing as he lost strength. He dripped blood, falling like raindrops below. He was weak from hunger, from his wounds, from the thousand jabs of spears he had received. He wanted to fly on, to find a target for destruction, but he felt his eyes closing, too heavy for him now. He felt himself drifting in and out of consciousness.

The dragon knew he was dying. In a way it was a relief; soon, he would join his father.

He was awakened by the sound of rustling leaves and cracking branches and as he felt himself smashing through treetops, he finally opened his eyes. His vision was obscured in a world of green. No longer able to control himself, he felt himself tumbling, snapping branches, each snap hurting him more.

He finally came to an abrupt stop high up in a tree, stuck between branches, too weak to struggle. He hung there, immobile, in too much pain to move, each breath hurting more than the next. He was sure he would die up here, tangled in the trees.

One of the branches suddenly gave with a loud snap, and the dragon plummeted. He tumbled end over end, snapping more branches, falling a good fifty feet, until finally he hit the ground.

He lay there, feeling all his ribs cracking, breathing blood. He flapped one wing slowly, but could not do much more.

As he felt the life force leaving him, it felt unfair, premature. He knew he had a destiny, but he could not understand what it was. It appeared to be short and cruel, born in this world only to witness his father's death, and then to die himself. Maybe that was what life was: cruel and unfair.

As he felt his eyes closing for the last time, the dragon found his mind filled with one final thought: *Father, wait for me. I will see you soon.*

CHAPTER SIX

Alec stood on the deck, gripping the rail of the sleek black ship, and watched the sea, as he had been for days. He watched the giant waves roll in and out, lifting their small sailing ship, and watched the foam break below the hold as they cut through water with a speed unlike anything he had ever experienced. Their ship leaned as the sails were stiff with wind, the gales strong and steady. Alec studied it with a craftsman's eyes, wondering what this ship was made of; clearly it was crafted of an unusual, sleek material, one he had never encountered before, and it had allowed them to maintain speed all day and night, and to maneuver in the dark past the Pandesian fleet, out of the Sea of Sorrow, and into the Sea of Tears.

As Alec reflected, he recalled what a harrowing journey it had been, a journey through days and nights, the sails never lowering, the long nights on the black sea filled with hostile sounds, of the ship's creaking, and of exotic creatures jumping and flapping. More than once he had awakened to see a glowing snake trying to board the boat, only to watch the man he was sailing with kick it off with his boot.

Most mysterious of all, more so than any of the exotic sea life, was Sovos, the man at the helm of the ship. This man who had sought Alec out at the forge, who had brought him on this ship, who was taking him to some remote place, a man Alec wondered if he were crazy to trust. Thus far, at least, Sovos had already saved Alec's life. Alec recalled looking back at the city of Ur as they were far out at sea, feeling agony, feeling helpless, as he witnessed the Pandesian fleet closing in. From the horizon, he had seen the cannonballs crack through the air, had heard the distant rumble, had seen the toppling of the great buildings, buildings which he himself had been inside but hours before. He had tried to get off the ship, to help them all, but by then, they had been too far away. He had insisted that Sovos turn around, but his pleas had fallen on deaf ears.

Alec teared up at the thought of all his friends back there, especially Marco and Dierdre. He closed his eyes and tried, to no avail, to shake away the memory. His chest tightened as he felt he had let them all down.

The only thing keeping Alec going, that shook him from his despondency, was the sense that he was needed elsewhere, as Sovos had insisted; that he had a certain destiny, that he could use it to help destroy the Pandesians somewhere else. After all, as Sovos had said, his dying back there with the rest of them would not have helped anyone. Still, he hoped and prayed that Marco and Dierdre had survived, and that he could still return in time to reunite with them.

So curious to know where they were going, Alec had peppered Sovos with questions, yet he had remained stubbornly silent, always at the helm night and day, his back to Alec. He never, as far as Alec could tell, even slept or ate. He just stood there watching the sea in his tall leather boots and black leather coat, his scarlet silks draped over his shoulder, wearing a cape with its curious insignia. With his short, brown beard and flashing green eyes that stared at the waves as if they were one with them, the mystery around him only deepened.

Alec stared out at the unusual Sea of Tears, with its light aqua color, and he felt overcome with an urgency to know where he was being taken. Unable to stand the silence any longer, he turned to Sovos, desperate for answers.

"Why me?" Alec asked, breaking the silence, trying yet again, determined this time for an answer. "Why choose me from that entire city? Why was *I* the one meant to survive? You could have saved a hundred people more important than me."

Alec waited, but Sovos remained silent, his back to him, studying the sea.

Alec decided to try another route.

"Where are we going?" Alec asked yet again. "And how is this ship able to sail so fast? What is it made of?"

Alec watched the man's back. Minutes passed.

Finally, the man shook his head, his back still turned.

"You are going where you are meant to go, where you are meant to be. I chose you because we need you, and no other."

Alec wondered.

"Need me for what?" Alec pressed.

"To destroy Pandesia."

"Why me?" Alec asked. "How can I possibly help?"

"All will be clear once we arrive," Sovos replied.

"Arrive where?" Alec pressed, frustrated. "My friends are in Escalon. People I love. A girl."

"I am sorry," Sovos sighed, "but no one is left back there. All that you once knew and loved is gone."

There came a long silence, and amidst the whistling of the wind, Alec prayed he was wrong—yet deep down he felt he was right. How could life change so quickly? he wondered.

"Yet you are alive," Sovos continued, "and that is a very precious gift. Do not squander it. You can help many others, if you pass the test."

Alec furrowed his brow.

"What test?" he asked.

Sovos finally turned and looked at him, his eyes piercing.

"If you are the one," he said, "our cause will fall on your shoulders; if not, we shall have no use for you."

Alec tried to understand.

"We've been sailing for days now and have gotten nowhere," Alec observed. "Just deeper into the sea. I can't even see Escalon anymore."

The man smirked.

"And where do you think we're going?" he asked.

Alec shrugged.

"It appears we sail northeast. Perhaps somewhere toward Marda."

Alec studied the horizon, exasperated.

Finally, Sovos replied.

"How wrong you are, young one," he replied. "How wrong indeed."

Sovos turned back to the helm as a strong gust of wind rose up, the boat riding into the whitecaps of the ocean. Alec look beyond him, and as he did, for the first time, he was startled to spot a shape on the horizon.

He hurried forward, filled with excitement as he gripped the rail.

In the distance there slowly emerged a landmass, just beginning to take shape. The land seemed to sparkle, as if made of diamonds. Alec raised a hand to his eyes, peering, wondering what it could possibly be. What island could exist out here in the middle of nowhere? He wracked his brain, but could remember no land on the maps. Was it some country he had never heard of?

"What is it?" Alec asked in a rush, staring out in anticipation.

Sovos turned, and for the first time since Alec had met him, he smiled wide.

"Welcome, my friend," he said, "to the Lost Isles."

CHAPTER SEVEN

Aidan stood bound to a post, unable to move, while he watched his father, kneeling a few feet before him, flanked by Pandesian soldiers. They stood, swords raised, holding them over his head.

"NO!" Aidan shrieked.

He tried to break free, to rush forward and spare his father, yet no matter how hard he tried, he could not budge, the ropes digging into his wrists and ankles. He was forced to watch as his father knelt there, eyes filled with tears, looking to him for help.

"Aidan!" his father called, reaching a hand out for him.

"Father!" Aidan called back.

The blades came down, and a moment later, Aidan's face was splattered in blood as they chopped off his father's head.

"NO!" Aidan shrieked, feeling his own life collapse within him, feeling himself sinking into a black hole.

Aidan woke with a start, gasping, covered in a cold sweat. He sat up in the darkness, struggling to realize where he was.

"Father!" Aidan yelled, still half asleep, looking for him, still feeling an urgency to save him.

He looked all around, felt something in his face and hair, all over his body, and realized it was hard to breathe. He reached out, pulled something light and long off his face, and he realized he was lying in a pile of hay, nearly buried in it. He quickly brushed it all off as he sat up.

It was dark in here, only the faint flicker of a torch appearing through slats, and he soon realized he was lying in the back of a wagon. Beside him came a rustling, and he looked over and saw with relief that it was White. The huge dog jumped up in the wagon beside him and licked his face, while Aidan hugged him back.

Aidan breathed hard, still overwhelmed by the dream. It had seemed too real. Had his father really been killed? He tried to think back to when he had last seen him, in the royal courtyard, ambushed, surrounded. He recalled trying to help, and then being whisked away by Motley in the thick of night. He recalled Motley putting him on this wagon, their riding through the backstreets of Andros to get away.

That explained the wagon. But where had they gone? Where had Motley taken him?

A door opened, and a sliver of torchlight lit up the dark room. Aidan was finally able to see where he was: a small stone room, the ceiling low and arched, looking like a small cottage or tavern. He looked up to see Motley standing in the doorway, framed in the torchlight.

"Keep yelling like that and the Pandesians will find us," Motley warned.

Motley turned and walked out, returning to the well-lit room in the distance, and Aidan quickly hopped down from the wagon and followed, White at his side. As Aidan entered the bright room, Motley quickly closed the thick oak door behind him and bolted it several times.

Aidan looked out, eyes adjusting to the light, and recognized familiar faces: Motley's friends. The actors. All those entertainers from the road. They were all here, all hiding away, boarded up in this windowless, stone pub. All the faces, once so festive, were now grim, somber.

"Pandesians are everywhere," Motley said to Aidan. "Keep your voice down."

Aidan, embarrassed, hadn't even realized he was shouting.

"Sorry," he said. "I had a nightmare."

"We all have nightmares," Motley replied.

"We're living in one," added another actor, his face glum.

"Where are we?" Aidan asked, looking around, puzzled.

"A tavern," Motley replied, "at the farthest corner of Andros. We are still in the capital, hiding out. The Pandesians patrol outside. They've walked by several times, but they haven't come in—and they won't, as long as you keep quiet. We're safe here."

"For now," called out one of his friends, skeptical.

Aidan, feeling an urgency to help his father, tried to remember.

"My father," he said. "Is he…dead?"

Motley shook his head.

"I don't know. He was taken. That was the last I saw him."

Aidan felt a flush of resentment.

"You took me away!" he said angrily. "You shouldn't have. I would have helped him!"

Motley rubbed his chin.

"And how would you have managed that?"

Aidan shrugged, wracking his brain.

"I don't know," he replied. "Somehow."

Motley nodded.

"You would have tried," he agreed. "And you would be dead now, too."

"Is he dead then?" Aidan asked, feeling his heart wrench within him.

Motley shrugged.

"Not when we left," Motley said. "I just do not know now. We have no friends, no spies, in the city anymore—it has been overtaken by Pandesians. All your father's men are imprisoned. We are, I'm afraid, at Pandesia's mercy."

Aidan clenched his fists, thinking only of his father rotting in that cell.

31

"I must save him," Aidan declared, filled with a sense of purpose. "I cannot let him sit there. I must leave this place at once."

Aidan jumped up and hurried to the door and had started pulling back the bolts when Motley appeared, stood over him, and stuck his foot before the door before he could open it.

"Go now," Motley said, "and you'll get us all killed."

Aidan looked back at Motley, saw a serious expression for the first time, and he knew he was right. He had a new sense of gratitude and respect for him; after all, he had indeed saved his life. Aidan would always be grateful for that. Yet at the same time, he felt a burning desire to rescue his father, and he knew that every second counted.

"You said there would be another way," Aidan said, remembering. "That there would be another way to save him."

Motley nodded.

"I did," Motley admitted.

"Were those just empty words, then?" Aidan asked.

Motley sighed.

"What do you propose?" he asked, exasperated. "Your father sits in the heart of the capital, in the royal dungeon, guarded by the entire Pandesian army. Shall we just go and knock on the door?"

Aidan stood there, trying to think of anything. He knew it was a daunting task.

"There must be men who can help us?" Aidan asked.

"Who?" called out one of the actors. "All those men loyal to your father were captured along with him."

"Not *all*," Aidan replied. "Surely some of his men were not there. What about the warlords loyal to him outside the capital?"

"Perhaps." Motley shrugged. "But where are they now?"

Aidan fumed, desperate, feeling his father's imprisonment as if it were his own.

"We can't just sit here and do *nothing*," Aidan exclaimed. "If you don't help me, I will go myself. I don't care if I die. I cannot just sit here while my father's in prison. And my brothers…" Aidan said, remembering, and he began to cry, overcome with emotion, as he recalled his two brothers' deaths.

"I have no one now," he said.

Then he shook his head. He remembered his sister, Kyra, and he prayed with all he had that she was safe. After all, she was all he had now.

As Aidan cried, embarrassed, White came over and rested his head against his leg. He heard heavy footsteps crossing the creaky, wooden plank floors, and he felt a big beefy palm on his shoulder.

He looked up and saw Motley looking down with compassion.

"Wrong," Motley said. "You have us. We are your family now."

32

Motley turned and gestured to the room, and Aidan looked out and saw all the actors and entertainers looking back at him earnestly, dozens of them, compassion in their eyes as they nodded in agreement. He realized that, even though they were not warriors, they were good-hearted people. He had a new respect for them.

"Thank you," Aidan said. "But you are all actors. What I need are warriors. You cannot help me get back my father."

Motley suddenly had a look in his eyes, as if an idea were dawning, and he smiled wide.

"How wrong you are, young Aidan," he replied.

Aidan could see Motley's eyes gleaming, and he knew he was thinking of something.

"Warriors have a certain skill," Motley said, "yet entertainers have a skill of their own. Warriors can win by force—but entertainers can win by other means, means even more powerful."

"I do not understand," Aidan said, confused. "You can't entertain my father out of his jail cell."

Motley laughed aloud.

"In fact," he replied, "I think I can."

Aidan looked back, puzzled.

"What do you mean?" he asked.

Motley rubbed his chin, his eyes drifting, clearly hatching a plan.

"Warriors are not allowed to walk freely in the capital now—or go anywhere near the city center. Yet entertainers have no restrictions."

Aidan was confused.

"Why would Pandesia let entertainers into the heart of the capital?" Aidan asked.

Motley smiled and shook his head.

"You still don't know how the world works, boy," Motley replied. "Warriors are always only allowed in limited places, and at limited times. But entertainers—they are allowed everywhere, at all times. Everybody always needs to be entertained, Pandesians as much as Escalonites. After all, a bored soldier is a dangerous soldier, on either side of the kingdom, and rule of order must be maintained. Entertainment has always been the key to keeping troops happy, and to controlling an army."

Motley smiled.

"You see, young Aidan," he said, "it is not the commanders who hold the keys to their armies, but us. Mere, old entertainers. Those of the class you despise so much. We rise above battle, cut across enemy lines. No one cares what armor I'm wearing—they care only how good my tales are. And I have fine tales, boy, finer than you shall ever know."

Motley turned to the room and boomed:

"We shall perform a play! All of us!"

All the actors in the room suddenly cheered, brightened, rising to their feet, hope returning to their dejected eyes.

"We shall perform our play right in the heart of capital! It shall be the greatest entertainment these Pandesians have ever seen! And more importantly, the greatest distraction. When the time is right, when the city is in our hands, captivated by our great performance, we shall act. And we shall find a way to free your father."

The men cheered and Aidan, for the first time, felt his heart warming, felt a new sense of optimism.

"Do you really think it will work?" Aidan asked.

Motley smiled.

"Crazier things, my boy," he said, "have happened."

CHAPTER EIGHT

Duncan tried to blot out the pain as he drifted in and out of sleep, lying back against the stone wall, the shackles cutting into his wrists and ankles and keeping him awake. More than anything, he craved water. His throat was so parched, he couldn't swallow, so raw that each breath hurt. He could not remember how many days it had been since he'd had a sip, and he felt so weak from hunger he could barely move. He knew he was wasting away down here, and that if the executioner didn't come for him soon, then hunger would take him.

Duncan drifted in and out of consciousness, as he had for days, the pain overwhelming him, becoming a part of who he was. He had flashes of his youth, of times spent in open fields, on training grounds, in battlefields. He had memories of his first battles, of days gone by, when Escalon was free and flourishing. These were always interrupted, though, by the faces of his two dead boys, rising up before him, haunting him. He was torn apart by agony, and he shook his head, trying unsuccessfully to make it all go away.

Duncan thought of his last remaining son, Aidan, and he desperately hoped he was safe back in Volis, that the Pandesians had not reached it yet. His mind then turned to thoughts of Kyra. He remembered her as a young girl, recalled the pride he had always taken in raising her. He thought of her journey across Escalon and he wondered if she had reached Ur, if she had met her uncle, if she was safe now. She was a part of him, the only part of him that mattered now, and her safety mattered more to him than being alive. Would he ever see her again? he wondered. He craved to see her, yet he also wanted her to remain far from here, and safe from all of this.

The cell door slammed open, and Duncan looked up, startled, as he peered into the darkness. Boots marched in the blackness, and as he listened to the gait, Duncan could tell they were not Enis's boots. In the darkness, his hearing had grown more acute.

As the soldier approached, Duncan figured he was coming to torture or kill him. Duncan was ready. They could do with him as they pleased—he had already died inside.

Duncan opened his eyes, heavy as they were, and looked up with whatever dignity he could muster to see who was coming. There, he was shocked to see, was the face of the man he despised the most: Bant of Barris. The traitor. The man who had killed his two sons.

Duncan glowered back as Bant stepped forward, a satisfied smirk on his face, and knelt before him. He wondered what this creature could possibly be doing here.

"Not so powerful now, are you, Duncan?" Bant asked, just feet away. He stood there, hands on hips, short, stocky, with narrow lips, beady eyes and a pockmarked face.

Duncan tried to lunge forward, wanting to tear him apart—but his chains held him back.

"You shall pay for my boys," Duncan said, choking up, his throat so dry he couldn't get out the words with the venom he wished.

Bant laughed, a short, crude sound.

"Shall I?" he mocked. "You'll be breathing your last dying breath down here. I killed your sons, and I can kill you, too, if I choose. I have the backing of Pandesia now, after my display of loyalty. But I shall not kill you. That would be too kind. Better to let you waste away."

Duncan felt a cold rage bubbling up within him.

"Then why you have come?"

Bant darkened.

"I can come for any reason I wish," he scowled, "or for no reason at all. I can come just to look at you. To gape at you. To see the fruits of my victory."

He sighed.

"And yet it so happens, I have a reason to visit you. There is something I wish from you. And there is one thing I am going to give you."

Duncan looked back skeptically.

"Your freedom," Bant added.

Duncan watched him, wondering.

"And why would you do that?" he asked.

Bant sighed.

"You see, Duncan," he said, "you and I are not so different. We are both warriors. In fact, you are a man I've always respected. Your sons deserved to be killed—they were reckless blowhards. But you," he said, "I've always respected. You should not be down here."

He paused, examining him.

"So this is what I will do," he continued. "You will publicly confess your crimes against our nation, and you shall exhort all citizens of Andros to concede to Pandesian rule. If you do this, then I shall see that Pandesia sets you free."

Duncan sat there, so furious he didn't know what to say.

"Are you a puppet for the Pandesians now?" Duncan finally asked, seething. "Are you trying to impress them? To show them that you can deliver me?"

Bant sneered.

"Do it, Duncan," he replied. "You are no good to anyone down here, least of all yourself. Tell the Supreme Ra what he wants to hear, confess what you've done, and make peace for this city. Our capital needs peace now, and you are the only who can make it."

Duncan took several deep breaths, until he finally summoned the strength to speak.

"Never," he replied.

Bant glowered.

"Not for my freedom," Duncan continued, "not for my life, and not for any price."

Duncan stared at him, smiling in satisfaction as he watched Bant redden, then finally he added: "But be sure of one thing: if I ever escape from here, my sword will find a spot in your heart."

After a long, stunned silence, Bant stood, scowling, stared down at Duncan, and shook his head.

"Live a few more days for me," he said, "so that I can be here to watch your execution."

CHAPTER NINE

Dierdre rowed with all her might, Marco beside her, the two of them swiftly cutting through the canal, making their way back toward the sea, where she had last seen her father. Her heart was torn apart with anxiety as she recalled the last time she had seen her father, recalled his bravely attacking the Pandesian army, even against insurmountable odds. She closed her eyes and shook away the image, rowing even faster, praying he was not dead yet. All she wanted was to make it back in time to save him— or if not, then to at least have a chance to die by his side.

Beside her, Marco rowed just as quickly, and she looked over at him with gratitude and wonder.

"Why?" she asked.

He turned and looked at her.

"Why did you join me?" she pressed.

He looked at her, silent, then looked away.

"You could have gone with the others back there," she added. "But you chose not to. You chose to come with me."

He looked straight ahead, still rowing hard, still remaining silent.

"Why?" she insisted, desperate to know, rowing furiously.

"Because my friend admired you very much," Marco said. "And that is enough for me."

Dierdre rowed harder, turning through the twisting canal, and her thoughts turned to Alec. She was so disappointed in him. He had abandoned them all, had departed Ur with that mysterious stranger before the invasion. Why? She could only wonder. He had been so devoted to the cause, the forge, and she was sure he'd be the last person to flee in a time of need. Yet he had, when they needed him most.

It made Dierdre reexamine her feelings for Alec, whom, after all, she barely knew—and it made her have stronger feelings for his friend Marco, who had sacrificed for her. Already she felt a strong bond with him. As cannonballs continued to whistle overhead, as buildings continued to explode and topple all around them, Dierdre wondered if Marco really knew what he was getting into. Did he know that by joining her, by returning into the heart of chaos, there would be no return?

"We row toward death, you know," she said. "My father and his men are on that beach, beyond that wall of rubble, and I intend to find him and fight by his side."

Marco nodded.

"Do you think I returned to this city to live?" he asked. "If I wanted to flee, I had my chance."

Satisfied, and touched by his strength, Dierdre rowed on, the two of them continuing silently, avoiding falling debris as they turned ever closer toward the shore.

Finally, they turned a corner, and in the distance she spotted the wall of rubble where she had last seen her father—and just beyond it, the tall black ships. She knew that on the other side lay the beach where he was battling the Pandesians, and she rowed with all she had, sweat pouring down her face, anxious to reach him in time. She heard the sounds of fighting, of men groaning out, dying, and she prayed it was not too late.

Barely had their boat reached the edge of the canal when she jumped out, rocking it, Marco behind her, and sprinted for the wall. She scrambled over the massive boulders, scraping her elbows and knees and not caring. Out of breath, she climbed and climbed, slipping on rocks, thinking only of her father, of having to reach the other side, hardly comprehending that these mounds of rubble were once the great towers of Ur.

She glanced over her shoulder as she heard the shouts, and, afforded a sweeping view of Ur from up here, she was shocked to see half the city in ruins. Buildings were toppled, mountains of rubble in the streets, covered by clouds of dust. She saw the people of Ur fleeing for their lives in every direction.

She turned back around and continued climbing, going the opposite direction of the people, wanting to embrace the battle—not run from it. She finally reached the top of the rock wall, and as she looked out, her heart stopped. She stood there, frozen in place, unable to move. This was not what she had expected at all.

Dierdre had expected to see a great battle being waged below, to see her father fighting valiantly, his men all around him. She expected to be able to rush down there and join him, to save him, to fight at his side.

Instead, what she saw made her want to curl up and die.

There lay her father, face-first in the sand, covered in a pool of blood, a hatchet in his back.

Dead.

All around him lay his dozens of soldiers, all dead, too. Thousands of Pandesian soldiers clamored off the ships like ants, spreading out, covering the beach, stabbing each body to make sure it was dead. They stepped on her father's body and the others as they made their way for the wall of rubble, and right for her.

Dierdre looked down as she heard a noise and saw some Pandesians had already reached it, were already climbing up, hardly thirty feet away, right for her.

Dierdre, filled with despair, anguish, rage, stepped forward and hurled her spear down at the first Pandesian she saw climbing up. He looked up, clearly not expecting to see anyone atop the wall, not expecting anyone to be crazy enough to face off against an invading army. Dierdre's spear impaled his chest, sending him sliding back down the rock and taking out several soldiers with him.

The other soldiers rallied, and a dozen of them raised their spears and threw them back up at her. It happened too quickly and Dierdre stood there defenseless, wanting to be impaled, ready to die. Wanting to die. She had been too late—her father was dead below, and now she, overwhelmed by guilt, wanted to die with him.

"Dierdre!" cried a voice.

Dierdre heard Marco beside her, and a moment later she felt him grabbing her, yanking her back down to the other side of the rubble. Spears whizzed by her head, right where she had been standing, missing her by inches, and she tumbled backwards, back down the pile of rubble, with Marco.

She felt terrible pain as the two of them tumbled head over heels, the rocks smashing her ribs, all over her body, bruising and scratching her all over the place, until finally they hit the bottom.

Dierdre lay there for a moment, struggling to breathe, feeling the wind knocked out of her, wondering if she were dead. She realized dimly that Marco had just saved her life.

Marco, quickly recovering, grabbed her and yanked her back to her feet. They ran together, stumbling, her body aching, away from the wall and back into the streets of Ur.

Dierdre glanced back over her shoulder and saw Pandesians already reaching the top. She watched as they raised bows and began to fire arrows, raining down death on the city.

All around Dierdre cries rang out as people began to fall, pierced in the back by arrows and spears as the sky turned black. Dierdre saw an arrow descending right for Marco and she reached out and yanked him, pulling him out of the way, behind a wall of rock. There came the sound of arrowheads hitting the stone behind them, and Marco turned and looked at her gratefully.

"We're even," she said.

There followed a shout, then a great clanging of armor, and she looked out to see dozens more Pandesians reach the top, all of them charging down the rock. Some were faster than others, and several of them, leading the pack, raced right for Dierdre.

Dierdre and Marco exchanged a knowing look, and nodded. Neither was prepared to run.

Marco stepped out from behind the rock as they neared, raised his spear, and aimed for the lead soldier. The spear lodged in his chest, dropping him.

Marco then spun around and slashed another's throat with his sword; he kicked a third soldier as he neared, then raised his sword high and brought it down on the fourth.

Dierdre, inspired, grabbed a flail from the ground and turned and swung with all her might. The spiked metal ball smashed an approaching soldier in the helmet, knocking him down, and she swung again and smashed another in the back before he could stab Marco.

The six soldiers dead, Marco and Dierdre exchanged a look, realizing how lucky they were. Yet all around them, the other citizens of Ur were not so lucky. More cannon fire whizzed overhead, and there followed explosion after explosion as more buildings were destroyed. At the same time, hundreds more soldiers appeared over the ridge, and as they began to pour through the city, citizens were stabbed and hacked in every direction.

Soon the streets, filled with bodies, ran with blood.

Dozens more soldiers charged for them, and Dierdre knew that she and Marco could not defend against them all. Just feet away, Dierdre braced herself as Pandesians, in their blue and yellow armor, raised swords and hatchets and bore down on them. She knew her life was about to end.

Just then, a cannonball smashed into a wall, and it toppled and blocked off the soldiers' approach, ironically crushing a few of them and creating a wall of defense. Dierdre breathed deep, realizing they had one last chance for survival.

"This way!" Marco shouted.

He grabbed her wrist and dragged her and they began to run through the city, weaving their way amidst the destruction. She knew that Marco knew the city better than anyone, and if they had any chance of survival, he would find it.

They twisted and turned down one street after the other, through clouds of dust, jumping over rubble, past dead bodies, avoiding bands of roving soldiers. Finally, Marco tugged her to a stop.

At first Dierdre was puzzled, seeing nothing; but then Marco bent down, wiped away some dust, and revealed in iron hatch hidden in the stone. He yanked it up, and Dierdre was amazed to see a hole leading underground.

Dierdre heard a noise and turned to see two Pandesians emerge from a cloud of dust, charging, axes raised high. Before she even had time to ponder it, Marco grabbed her and yanked her down—and she shrieked as she went falling belowground, hurling somewhere into the blackness.

CHAPTER TEN

Kyra opened her eyes as she felt a tremendous warmth radiate throughout her body, feeling like the heat of the sun were spreading through her. Her eyes were heavy, and as she was met by a world of white light, it took her a moment to realize where she was. She raised her hand to the morning sun, breaking through the trees, a new dawn spreading over the wood, and she had never experienced such a feeling of peace.

As Kyra felt the heat coursing through her, she looked down at her stomach and was amazed to see her wound was mostly healed. She ran a finger over it, stunned: her skin was almost smooth.

Kyra looked up as she sensed motion, and she saw a face. She was thrilled to see those intense, shining eyes looking down at her, fixed on hers.

Kyle.

He knelt over her, holding her hand, and as she looked into his eyes, she felt as if they held the power of the sun. She felt waves of heat coursing through his palm, into hers, making her more and more sleepy. Her eyes were so heavy, not fully open, as though she couldn't quite cast off her heavy slumber.

She smiled, reassured by his presence, feeling such a wave of love and gratitude toward him.

"You're still here," she said, her voice soft, in a dreamlike state.

"Shh," he said, looking down, running a soft hand through her hair. "You must sleep. The wound was deep. But it is healing now. My time here is done."

She looked up, feeling a sudden rush of concern.

"Are you leaving me?" she asked, panicked, feeling so alone in the world.

He smiled down at her.

"My tower is in danger," he replied. "My people need me now."

There was so much Kyra wanted to ask him, but she couldn't find the words. Her mind was still in a haze, and her exhaustion deepened with every moment.

"Stay," she whispered.

But exhaustion overcame her, and as Kyle placed a palm on her eyes, a tremendous heat forced them closed.

Kyra felt herself getting lighter, shifting into white light, drifting back to sleep. The last thing she remembered, before her eyes closed completely, was Kyle removing his necklace, a startling star-shaped sapphire, and draping it over her neck. She felt its cool healing power on her collarbone.

"What's mine is yours now," he said. "Sleep. And remember me."

*

Kyra sat bolt upright. She opened her eyes to see the sun high overhead, and she blinked in the brightness, looking everywhere for Kyle.

As she feared, he was gone.

Kyra jumped to her feet, feeling a rush of energy, amazed to be standing. She felt stronger than ever. She looked down at her stomach, where her wound had been, and was amazed to see it was entirely healed. It was as if nothing had ever happened.

Kyra stood there, feeling reborn, and as she heard a whining she turned to see Leo by her side, licking her palm. She heard a grunt, and she turned to see Andor, in the near distance, pawing the ground. She was still in a forest clearing, light flooding through the trees, wind rustling the leaves, the sounds of birds and insects filling the air. She felt as if she were seeing the world with new eyes. She took a deep breath, loving what it felt like to be alive again.

There came a rustling, and Kyra turned and was startled to see Alva standing a few feet away, expressionless, holding his staff and watching her silently. She felt a deep sense of relief at the sight of him, yet also guilt. He had warned her not to go, and she had not heeded him. Here she was, the failed student, she felt, facing her teacher. She burned with questions for him.

"How long have you been here?" she asked, sensing he had watched over her during her sleep.

He did not respond.

"Have you been watching me all this time?" she asked.

"I am always watching you."

Kyra tried to remember.

"Was it Kyle who healed me?" she asked.

He nodded.

"I was meant to die, wasn't I?" she asked. "He sacrificed himself for me, didn't he?"

"Indeed," he replied. "And he will pay the price."

Kyra felt a sudden rush of concern.

"What price?"

"There is a price to everything in this universe, Kyra. Destiny cannot be changed without the greatest price of all."

She felt a stab of fear.

"I do not wish for him to pay a price for my life," she replied.

Alva sighed, looking sad, disappointed.

43

"I warned you," he replied. "Your haste, your action, has harmed others. Courage is selfless, and yet sometimes it can be selfish, too."

Kyra thought about that.

"You did not heed my words," Alva continued. "You abandoned your training. You thought of no one but your father. If it weren't for Kyle, and for…."

Alva trailed off and looked away, and Kyra suddenly knew.

"My mother," she said, her eyes lighting. "That's what you were about to say, wasn't it?"

He looked away.

"I saw her in my dream," she pressed, and rushed toward Alva and grabbed his arm, desperate to know more. "I saw her face. She was healing me. She helped change my destiny."

Kyra prayed that Alva would answer her. She was overcome with a primal need to know more about her mother, a need as strong as food or drink

"Please," she added. "I have to know."

"Yes," he finally replied, to her immense relief, "she did."

"You must tell me," she said. "Tell me everything about her."

Alva stared back for a long time, his eyes twinkling, clearly holding some great knowledge. He looked as if he were pondering whether to tell her.

"Please," Kyra implored. "I nearly died. I have earned the right to know. I cannot go down to my death without knowing. Who is she?"

Finally, Alva sighed. He took a few steps away, casting off her hand, and with his back to her, stared off into the trees, as if peering into different worlds.

"Your mother was one of the Ancients," he finally began, his voice deep, rumbling. "One of the first people to inhabit Escalon. They are those who are said to have been born before anyone else, beings who are said to have lived for thousands of years, who were never meant to die. They were stronger than us, stronger than the trolls—stronger even than the dragons. They were the first people. The original people."

Kyra listened, mesmerized.

"Because of their power, their strength," Alva continued, "Escalon was never invaded. They were the ones that fended them off, that created the Flames, that built the towers, that forged the Sword of Fire. Because of them, the dragons were kept at bay. Their power protected us all."

Alva turned and looked at her meaningfully, as Kyra stood there, riveted.

"A power that runs through you, Kyra," he said.

She felt a chill at his words.

44

"Where is she, then?" Kyra asked, her voice nearly a whisper. "Does she still live?"

Alva looked away and sighed. He fell silent for a long time.

"One of her kind turned to the wrong side," he said, sadness in his voice. "He used his power in the wrong ways. His energy turned dark, uncontrollable. From him there is said to have spawned the troll race."

Alva turned and looked at her, eyes shining with intensity.

"Don't you see, Kyra?" he pressed. "The trolls of Marda are descended from your kind, from the blood that runs through you. We are waging not only a war of soldiers, of men. This is a war of races, ancient races, ancient bloodlines. And it is a war of dragons. It is a war that has been raging for thousands of years, and that has never really stopped. It is a war of forces you can never understand. And your mother is at the center of it. Which means you are, too."

Kyra frowned, struggling to comprehend.

"You must train, Kyra," he insisted. "Not to learn how to wield a spear—but to understand this ancient energy that flows through you, that controls all. To understand who you are."

"Is my mother alive?" She was almost afraid to ask.

Alva looked at her for a long time, then shook his head.

"You may see her only in dreams, or not at all. You are too young yet. Not until you know more about yourself, your source of power. Your mother's source of power."

She wondered.

"Where can I find that?" she asked.

He looked at her for a long time, then finally, he replied:

"The Lost Temple."

The Lost Temple. The words shocked her, ringing in her ears like a mantra. It was a mysterious place she had heard of only in myths and legends. Yet the second he mentioned it, it resonated within her and she knew he was right.

"Once the capital of Escalon," he continued, "the seat of power for thousands of years. Now it lies an ancient ruin, nestled against the sea on the western coast. It is there you will find her, Kyra. And there, and there alone, you will discover the weapon you need. The only weapon that can save Escalon."

"What weapon?" she asked, amazed.

But Alva merely looked away.

Kyra felt a sudden flash of concern.

"My father," she wondered. "Is he…dead?"

Alva shook his head.

"Not yet," he replied. "He remains captive, in Andros. Until his execution."

45

Kyra felt a chill at his words, and she stood there, debating.

"Go to him," he warned, "and you will die. The choice is yours, Kyra: will you choose your family, or your destiny?"

Kyra looked up to the sky, wondering, feeling so confused, so torn. The world seemed to freeze at that moment.

When she looked back at Alva, to her shock, he was gone. She blinked, looking everywhere, finding no one.

There came a rustling behind her, and Kyra turned and was shocked to see Kolva standing there, having emerged from the woods, looking back at her with intensity. It was amazing seeing his face, the resemblance it bore to hers; in some ways, it was like looking in a mirror. It made her think of her mother, and his connection to her, all the more. Her other uncle was the last person she had expected to see, and yet he came as a very welcome face, especially now, as she grappled with the decision before her.

"What are you doing here?" Kyra asked. "I thought you had gone to the tower."

"I have already returned," he replied. "The tower is but one cog in a great wheel, a battlefield in a greater war. War is coming, Kyra, and I am needed elsewhere now."

"Where?" she asked, surprised.

He sighed.

"A place far from here," he replied. "Some battles must be lost," he added cryptically, "for others to be won."

She wondered what he meant.

"Why did you leave me?" she pressed.

"You were in good hands with your other uncle," he replied. "You needed time to train."

"And now that my training is over?" she asked.

He shook his head.

"It is never over," he replied. "Do not ever imagine that it is. That is when you will begin to fall."

Kyra frowned, debating.

"I am faced with a big decision," she said, eager for his advice.

"I know," he replied.

She looked at him with surprise.

"You do?" she asked.

He nodded.

"You want to save your father," he replied.

Kyra looked him over.

"He is your brother, after all," she said. "Why do you not rush to save him?"

Kolva sighed.

"I would if I could."

"And why can't you?" she asked.

"My mission is urgent," he replied. "I can't be in both places."

"But I can," she said.

He slowly shook his head.

"Did you not listen to Alva?" he asked. "Your mission is urgent, too. Your mother, my sister, awaits you."

Kyra felt torn, not knowing what to do.

"Are you saying then that I should abandon my father?" she asked.

"I am saying you are lucky to be alive," he said. "And if you do not achieve the power you need to first, then death will find you. And that will not help anyone."

He stepped in and laid a hand on her shoulder, and looked down with approving eyes.

"I am proud of you, Kyra," he said.

She wondered.

"Will we meet again?" she asked, feeling a pang at the idea of losing him, the only living relative she felt she had left.

"I hope so," he replied.

And then, without another word, he turned and hiked back into the forest, leaving Kyra alone, upset, and more confused than before.

As she stood there, not knowing how much time had passed, Andor finally snorted and looked right at her. Slowly, she felt a new feeling; it was her destiny rising up within her. Finally blessed with a sense of certainty for the first time, she came to a decision.

She crossed the clearing, mounted Andor, and sat there for a long time, until finally, she knew there was only one place she could go.

"Let us go, Andor," she said. "To the Lost Temple."

CHAPTER ELEVEN

Merk slid down the rope so fast he could barely breathe, flying down the side of the Tower of Ur, aiming for the army of waiting trolls below. He knew this plunge was suicidal, yet he no longer cared. With the tower surrounded, his fellow watchers nearly all dead, he was going to go down his way—not cowering at the top, but fighting hand-to-hand, just the way he always had in life, and taking some of them down with him.

The ground rushed up to meet him, and Merk, breathless, landed on the shoulders of two trolls, knocking them flat on their back and cushioning his own fall. He hit the ground ready, rolling and extracting two daggers from his waist, the same daggers he had used to assassinate his entire life, and he threw himself into the group of trolls.

He sliced one's throat with the dagger in his right hand, then reached backwards and stabbed another in the head behind him, fighting his own way. He stabbed one troll in the heart, another in the temple, and another in the gut. As they came at him with their huge halberds, swinging with enough power to chop off his head, he ducked and weaved, much lighter than they were, unencumbered by weapons and armor, then rose and slashed their throats. They all had one disadvantage: they were warriors, but he was an assassin. They were powerful, yet he was quick. None matched his agility.

Merk's greatest advantage was his use of distance. They needed to swing mighty weapons, yet he needed only to get close, inches away, to slice their throats. When he was in so close, they could not reach him with their weapons, and his small dagger gave him more advantage than their huge halberds would ever have. Merk ducked and weaved through the crowd like a fish, dropping trolls on all sides, knowing it was reckless, knowing his flank was unprotected, and knowing he could die at any moment. Yet he felt liberated in his charge, no longer fearing death.

Soon, though, the stunned army of trolls caught up with him. They surrounded him and closed in, and Merk suddenly felt a tremendous blow on his back; as he fell sideways, he realized he had been struck by a war hammer. He rolled on the ground, clutching his shoulder, dropping one of his daggers, and he looked up to see a massive, hideous troll, the one that had struck him, raising his war hammer high, about to smash it into his face.

Merk rolled out of the way as the hammer came down, just missing him and leaving a crater in the earth beside his head. The troll roared, raising it again, and Merk kicked him behind one knee, dropping him to the ground; he then leapt to his feet and raised his remaining dagger, plunging it into the back of his neck. The troll dropped face first, dead.

The move left Merk exposed, though, and his head rang as a huge shield smashed his head, knocking him to the ground. He rolled on the ground, seeing stars, his head pounding, then looked up to see another halberd being lowered for his head.

Merk again rolled out of the way right before it hit, then jumped to his feet and slashed this troll across the throat, killing it too.

Merk spun in every direction, breathing hard, unwilling to give up as the trolls closed in. Yet hundreds more arrived by the moment, and he knew this was a battle he could not win. He kept backing up until he was against the tower wall, nowhere left to run.

Suddenly there came a commotion, and Merk was confused as the trolls turned away from him and all looked up at the tower walls. He turned and looked up, too, and he was stunned by what he saw: the walls of the tower, which he had always assumed to be solid stone, suddenly opened up, and secret openings appeared in them, on every floor. Out of these appeared the glowing, intense yellow eyes of the ancient Watchers, their pale faces staring down at the trolls.

They slowly reached out with long, bony fingers, and as they did, Merk saw something shining and yellow their palms. They appeared to be orbs of light.

The Watchers turned their palms downward and Merk watched in awe as the orbs of light were hurled down at the trolls, leaving streaks in the sky. They hit the ground and moments later, explosions rang out.

All around Merk, trolls were killed by the dozen, torn to pieces and falling into the craters in the earth left by these orbs of light. The Watchers hurled down the orbs one after the other, and within moments, hundreds of trolls were dead.

Vesuvius emerged from the crowd. He held his huge golden shield high, and as he did, it deflected the orbs of light, leaving him unharmed, the shield clearly forged of some magic material. At the same time, Vesuvius reached back, grabbed a spear appearing to be crafted of gold, and hurled it at one of the Watchers.

There came an awful screech, a sound like the very fabric of the universe tearing apart, and Merk was pained to see a Watcher, a spear through his heart, began to shrivel up and melt before him. He slumped sideways over the window, lifeless.

Vesuvius's elite trolls stepped forward, all holding the golden shields and spears, and one at a time, they defended against the orbs and hurled their golden spears. One at a time, the ancient, precious Watchers fell.

Soon, the orbs of light stopped hurling down, leaving the tower truly defenseless. Worse, there came a great rustling in the wood, and Merk was horrified to see hundreds more trolls appear.

Merk felt a crushing pain in his lower kidney, and as he dropped to one knee, he realized he had been clubbed in the back. Gasping for breath, he looked up to see a troll swinging the club down for his head. He tried to dodge, but the pain was so severe that he moved too slowly; before he could get out of the way, he was clubbed again, in the back of the head, and he fell face first to the dirt.

Merk lay there, immobile, the pain throbbing in his kidneys and head, unable to breathe, much less move. The troll stepped forward with the club, a vicious smile on his face, and raised it high.

"Say good night, human."

Merk saw his life flash before his eyes; he knew that it would crush him, that he would die here, in this spot, in the mud, killed by this nation of trolls. In his mind there flashed images of the life he had led, the people he had killed, the choices he had made. Somehow, he felt he deserved this. Yet he was also in the midst of trying to change, to become a better person, and he felt he was almost there. He just needed a bit more time. He wasn't ready to die just yet. Why did his life have to end now, of all times? And why here, in the mud, at the hands of these grotesque beasts, while defending the only place he had ever cared for, while doing good for the first time in his life?

Merk braced himself for the blow, but to his amazement, it did not come. He looked up and heard a gasp. He was baffled as he saw a sapphire spear protruding through the troll's chest. The troll stood there, frozen, then dropped to the ground beside him, dead.

Merk looked up, wondering, and was confused by what he saw. A lone boy cut through the crowd, wielding the sapphire spear, slashing and dropping trolls in every direction. He was a dizzying blur of light, and it took Merk a minute to focus on him. He saw the long, golden hair, and he knew: Kyle. He had come back for him.

Kyle cut through the army of trolls like a whirlwind, killing three before one could turn to face him. None could even get close.

Yet the forest continued to open up, hundreds more trolls poured in, and soon it seemed there were too many even for Kyle, who, breathing hard, covered in blood, began to slow down. Merk watched as Kyle received a slice from a halberd on his arm, and he knew his time was running out. He watched in horror as Kyle then received another blow, a hatchet to his back. Merk called out as Kyle stumbled and fell, appearing dead.

But then, even more incredibly, the wound healed before Merk's eyes. Kyle rose to his feet again, wheeled, and faced the troll who had struck him, and instead he killed the beast.

With hundreds more trolls filtering in, Kyle suddenly turned to Merk. A moment later he felt Kyle's strong, bony hands grabbing him, lifting him

50

into the air, then over his shoulder. In too much pain to move, Merk realized that if Kyle had not come for him, he would surely have died here.

Moments later they were racing through the army of trolls, Kyle dodging and weaving, moving so fast that all the hatchets whizzed past them. Kyle ran faster, it seemed, than even the speed of light, as if he were running on air, and Merk could hardly breathe as he felt the world rush past. Soon they gained distance on the trolls, and were deep in the woods, heading south, the tower quickly fading into the distance.

"The tower," Merk mumbled, "we cannot leave it."

"It is already finished," replied Kyle.

"Then…where are we going?" Merk struggled to ask, his eyes closing as they ran.

"Far, far away from here."

CHAPTER TWELVE

Vesuvius led the charge as his trolls smashed the battering ram again and again into the golden doors of the Tower of Ur, each collision making the ground shake. The thick iron ram was bending the door a bit more each time. They were getting closer with each and every smash. Vesuvius was so close now to his dream, to getting the Sword, lowering the Wall of Flames, taking down the only barrier left between Marda and Escalon, he could taste it. It all lay just beyond those doors. With all the humans dead, and with those last two fleeing far away, nothing stood in his way now.

Yet still the door would not give.

Vesuvius, in a fit of rage, stepped forward and swung his halberd, lopping off the heads of two of the trolls pushing the ram. The other trolls looked up at him in terror.

"FASTER!" he commanded.

Two more trolls stepped forward to take their place and all the trolls rushed forward with even more speed, putting their entire bodies into it as they rammed it again and again, this time with greater force. Vesuvius got behind them and helped, pushing with his shoulders, his legs digging into the mud, straining with all he had.

"FORWARD!" he cried.

Finally, after one hard push, the ancient doors quaked and bent, then finally burst open, swinging wildly off their hinges. There came a tremendous explosion, sounding like metal being torn to shreds.

A shout rose up amongst the trolls as Vesuvius charged into the Tower of Ur, leading the way. He could hardly believe it. Here he was, charging into the one place he had always hoped to enter, the one place that legend had told could never be broken into. He had destroyed the doors that legend said could never be destroyed.

Vesuvius rushed into the cool, dim tower, his boots squeaking on its golden floors, his hundreds of trolls cheering behind him, all of them rushing up the immense spiral staircase together. As he looked up, Vesuvius saw a few remaining human soldiers rush down the spiral staircase, right for him. He snarled, raised his halberd, and killed these humans two at a time, sending them flying over the railing and hurling down below.

A few of the humans put up a fight, even managing to kill several of his trolls; yet more and more of his trolls flooded in behind him, overrunning the place, overwhelming the soldiers, and they were quickly killed.

Vesuvius ran up the stairs, taking them three at a time, leading his men. The rumble of their boots filled the tower like thunder, hundreds of trolls ascending the steps that were not meant to be ascended. Vesuvius nearly trembled with excitement, realizing how close he was, how soon the Sword of Fire would be in his hands.

He ascended flight after flight of this mysterious tower, and he looked at its mysterious carvings, the ancient floors and walls, made of an exotic material, each floor so different from the one before it. He made a mental to note himself that, after he finished stealing the Sword and any other valuables, he would burn this place to the ground. He hated beauty. He would leave nothing here but a pile of stones—and he would burn even that.

Vesuvius heard a commotion and he looked up and saw several more soldiers appearing from hidden rooms in the tower and rushing for him. He dodged as one swung for his head, and smashed him with his shield, sending him over the rail. He stabbed another in the gut with the point of his halberd, then swung around and chopped off the head of another, sending him tumbling down the staircase.

Up and up he went, floor after floor, leading his trolls, until finally he reached the end and burst through to the roof. There, finally under open sky, he was delighted to see dozens of dead humans, all murdered by his spears and arrows and catapults. Some lay wounded, groaning, and Vesuvius walked over to each one and stabbed them slowly, reveling in their cruel deaths.

On the far side of the roof, though, a dozen or so human soldiers remained, bloody, wounded, yet still approaching to fight. These men just would not quit. They raced for Vesuvius and he rushed forward, relishing the battle to come.

Vesuvius chopped one in the chest, swinging with his halberd before the man could reach him; he then dodged the sloppy sword slash of another soldier, spun around and stabbed him in the back. He raised his halberd high and turned it sideways, blocking a sword slash coming down at him, then kicked the soldier in the chest, raised his halberd high and chopped him in half.

All around him his trolls rushed forward and attacked the remaining humans left and right. The last one alive panicked, desperate, and turned and ran for the battlements. Vesuvius did not want to let him off so easily. He took aim, threw his spear, and it lodged in the man's back. Vesuvius grinned as he stepped forward slowly, grabbed the man from behind, and hurled him over the edge. He watched with great joy as fell shrieking, flailing, to his death below.

Vesuvius's trolls cheered, the tower finally theirs.

Vesuvius stood there, feeling a rush of victory. Never in his wildest dreams had he imagined he would be standing here, atop the tower, it entirely in his possession, the humans' most precious building. He felt as if nothing could stop him. As if the world were his.

Remembering the Sword, Vesuvius turned and rushed back down the stairs until he reached the top floor of the tower, the floor, legend had it, that held the mythical Sword. He put his shoulder into an oak door, smashing it open, then barreled through the chamber until he came to another door. He was puzzled to find a dead human lying at its entrance, the body cold, dead long ago. He was puzzled by that. Someone had been here already, had killed this human. But who? Why?

Vesuvius stepped forward in the silence, the shouts of the trolls muted behind the thick stone walls, and he pushed open the door, his heart pounding in anticipation. He entered the solemn chamber, lit dimly by torches, and as he looked up, he saw an ancient cradle of steel, velvet cushions beneath it, as if meant to hold the Sword. Vesuvius sensed immediately that he had found it.

He stepped forward, his heart pounding, expecting to see the Sword, to finally, after all this time, grasp it in his hands.

There, beneath the steel cradle, was a flaming torch, as if to signify this was the home of the Sword of Fire. Yet as Vesuvius slowly looked up, his heart fell. He felt a rush of devastation, of despair. It was as if the whole world had fooled him.

It was empty.

In a rage, Vesuvius rushed forward and smashed the cradle, swinging his halberd, destroying it again and again. He grabbed what was left, lifted it high overhead and hurled it into the walls, smashing it repeatedly. He finally leaned back and shrieked, and the sound shook the very fabric of the tower.

His journey through Escalon, he realized, had not even begun. There would   be   much   more   killing   ahead   of   him.

CHAPTER THIRTEEN

Anvin slowly peeled open one eye and managed to look out, just enough, to see a world of dust and death. His one good eye was encased with dust and dirt, and he opened it just a bit, the world but a sliver, and as he lay there, face-first in the desert rock, he desperately tried to remember where he was, what had happened. His limbs ached more than he thought possible, his body weighed a million tons, and he felt more dead than alive.

Anvin heard a distant rumble and he looked up to the horizon and could see the faint outline of an army, gleaming yellow and blue, marching away. They stirred up a cloud of dust as they marched north, away from him.

Slowly, he began to remember. The invasion. The Pandesians. The Southern Gate. Duncan had never arrived. He and his men had lost. They had failed to stop them.

Anvin lay there, feeling the bruises all over his body, the welts on his head, the cuts and wounds stinging. He felt a tremendous throbbing in his hand and he looked down to see his pinky finger was missing, the blood dried up, only a stump now. The memories came rushing back. The battle. The hordes of the world descending upon him at once.

Anvin wondered how he could be alive. He tried to look around, still unable to move his neck, and saw the dead face of Durge, lying but a few feet away, eyes wide open, staring back. The stern look haunted him, as if even in death Durge was saying *I told you so*.

Anvin shifted, just enough to look further and see the dead bodies of all his fellow soldiers, all the men who had followed him, who had believed in him, who had fought for Duncan, who had fought for Durge, all lying there, dead. He, apparently, was the sole survivor.

In flashes, Anvin recalled their glorious last stand. None of his men had backed down from the hordes of the world. Anvin recalled killing a dozen Pandesians as they reached him. It had been a glorious stand in the face of certain death. One in which he was meant to die, in which all of them were meant to die, and all of them had. Except him. Somehow, fate had been cruel, and had left him alive, he and he alone.

Anvin struggled to think back, to remember how he had survived. He remembered being smashed in the head with a hammer, it knocking him to the ground; then, horses stampeding over him. He shifted and felt the welts on his back where the horses, then the soldiers, had marched over him, all assuming him dead. Somehow he had been overlooked in the carnage as the army had marched over him. They'd assumed he was dead. And from the way he was feeling now, they weren't entirely wrong. A million welts and bruises. As he tried to move, he realized the pain was too intense.

Why had he lived to bear witness to this? Anvin wondered. Why couldn't he have died in one final glorious stand, as he had intended. What was the point of living now? Escalon was overrun. Surely everyone he knew and loved was dead. Duncan, too, must be dead; otherwise, he would have arrived to reinforce him.

Anvin used all his effort to move his arms out a little, and then, slowly, to pull himself up just a bit. He reached out, grabbed rock and dirt, and making a fist between his fingers, hands shaking, struggled to rise. He then reached out with the other arm, in pure agony, half his body unable to move. He had never experienced pain like this, had never been beaten and trampled by thousands of men. Hardly able to breathe, he rolled to his side, put one palm flat, and pushed himself up, just enough.

Slowly, he was able to lift his neck a bit more, his breath catching in his throat. His other eye was still sealed shut, yet somehow he made it to one knee, wobbling, nearly falling.

After minutes of sitting there, breathing hard, he forced himself to try again. He could not just die here. He had to go on.

Be strong.

Anvin looked over at Durge's dead body and saw his sword laying in the dust, just a few feet away. Anvin reached out, knowing it was the only way.

With a supreme effort, he managed to grab his friend's sword. Grabbing the hilt, he stuck it into the dirt and used it to steady himself as he rose up. Fitting, he thought, that he should bear Durge's sword.

With shaking arms Anvin made it to his feet. He stood there, unsteady, trying to balance. He breathed for a long time, not feeling as if he could go on. He was dizzy, wishing he could hold onto something, and he squinted into the sunset as he looked around with his one good eye. He wished he hadn't. He was surrounded by death, by desolation, realized he stood completely alone in this desert wasteland. Yet at least he was alive. He should be grateful for that.

Anvin turned and looked out at the horizon, at the disappearing Pandesian army invading Escalon, and he felt filled with resolve. He could not let them enter his country. Not after all he had stood for.

Somehow he mustered the energy to put one foot out before the other, and he took his first step.

Then another.

And another.

Anvin felt as if he were walking underwater, sweating, feeling as if he would collapse at any moment. He forced himself to think of Duncan, of all those back there that he knew and loved—and he forced himself to go on.

It would be an endless trek, he knew, a wasteland before him, and beyond that, the Pandesian army. Even if he made it, even if he reached them, he would surely be killed.

Yet he had no choice but to move forward.

That was who he was.

And that was what he lived for.

His whole life had been a forge, a forge of valor. And he was the man, the soldier, that his friends, his commanders, and most of all, himself, had forged. Each choice had forged him, had made him the person that he was, had shaped his character. And each choice mattered as much as the next one.

It was a choice to go on. Or a choice to retreat, to die here, to fail.

Anvin gripped his sword, clenched his teeth, and stepped forward, one foot a time. He had made his choice. He would survive, regardless of what life had thrown at him. He was stronger than hardship. Stronger than suffering.

And he would not stop until he had killed them all.

CHAPTER FOURTEEN

Dierdre cried out as she fell, plummeting down into the blackness, somewhere beneath the streets of Ur. She held tight to Marco's hand as they both descended, expecting the fall to kill her. She could not think of a more awful way to die.

Finally, she landed with a splash in a pool of water, up to her waist, immersed in freezing water. Marco landed with a splash beside her, and Dierdre, breathing hard, wiped water from her eyes and gasped for air, marveling that she was alive. Heart slamming, she looked around and saw that they had, at least, sealed themselves in underground, had spared themselves from a certain death above. Yet where were they?

She looked around in the dim light, getting her bearings, while Marco took her arm and helped her up. These tunnels were lit only by small shafts of sunlight coming in from somewhere high above, allowing just enough light for Dierdre to see water dripping from the rotting stone walls, the pools of water beneath her. Marco began to walk and she walked with him, still smarting from the fall and from the shock of how close she had come to dying up there.

Dierdre heard, high above, the thunder of the Pandesians storming the city, spreading out across Ur, killing all her people. She could hear the muffled screams even from way down here, screams of her fellow countrymen being killed, rising up with the echo of cannon fire, of buildings collapsing. She felt as if the world had come to an end.

Her heart banged with fear as directly above, she heard the sound of halberds pounding metal; clearly the Pandesians were trying to smash the hatch and pursue them down here.

"We must keep moving!" Marco urged, yanking her along.

Dierdre let him guide her, and they hurried through the tunnels, water splashing beneath their feet. She closed her eyes as she went, seeing flashes of her father's dead body back there on the beach, and trying to shake it away. It was almost too much to go on.

Marco, knowing these tunnels well, soon led her to a passage. They turned down another tunnel, echoing as they ran, then down another, until finally Marco led them to a small set of stone stairs, leading up. They ascended and Dierdre found herself in another tunnel, this one with a dry floor, closer to the surface, a bit brighter in here.

Marco suddenly pulled Dierdre into a corner and put his hand on her lips to quiet her. She stood beside him, barely breathing, and as Marco pointed to a shaft of sunlight high above, she looked up. Dierdre saw, through slats in the iron, Pandesian soldiers rushing back and forth; she saw people getting stabbed, falling everywhere, while others tried to flee. She looked over as Marco pointed, and on the far side of the tunnel saw a ladder leading up.

Dierdre felt a rush of outrage.

"We must save them!" Dierdre urged. "We cannot let them die!"

Marco's face was grim.

"To go up there would mean our death," he replied.

She frowned.

"Better to die helping those people than stay down here and die like cowards," she retorted.

Without thinking, Dierdre rushed to the ladder and climbed two rungs at a time until she reached the top, determined to save them. She immediately heard Marco behind her, climbing the ladder too, and as she reached the last rung, unable to pull back the heavy iron, she expected him to try to stop her, to pull her back down.

But to her surprise, Marco reached up and unlocked it. He hung there beside her, so close, and he stared back at her, love and admiration in his eyes. And then, to her surprise, he leaned forward and kissed her.

And to her even greater surprise, she leaned in and kissed him back. It was the kiss of two people who knew they were about to die, and had nothing left to lose.

Marco reached up and pushed the hatch gently, just enough to see a wave of Pandesian soldiers rushing past. They ran amidst dust and rubble, racing through the streets, chasing victims. Dierdre watched as a huge, arched building collapsed, blocking the way with a mountain of rubble, and, she was happy to see, killing several Pandesians in the process.

She spotted several citizens cowering behind the wall of rubble—old men, women, children—cut off from the pursuing Pandesians for the time being. But already she could hear the Pandesians climbing the wall.

"Now!" Dierdre cried.

She and Marco pushed open the latch all the way, and Dierdre burst back above ground, onto the streets, Marco beside her. She felt vulnerable up here, yet liberated, driven by a purpose.

As she reached them, the cowering people looked up at her with startled faces; Dierdre, wasting no time, grabbed the first one she saw, a child, perhaps ten, who looked up at her in fear.

"Come this way!" she said. "Quickly!"

All the people, seeing a chance for safety, followed her and Marco, racing for the open hatch. She and Marco guided them down the ladder, below ground, into the tunnels.

Dierdre looked up and saw the Pandesians begin to surface atop the mound of rubble, yet she did not descend. She stood there, refusing to descend until all the people were safely below.

"Go below!" Marco shouted to Dierdre, over the sound of a cannonball striking another building. He turned and held a spear at the ready, facing the Pandesians, standing guard, too, while more people descended. "It's too dangerous for you up here!"

She shook her head.

"Not until they're all down," she insisted.

There remained about a dozen more people—an old woman, a man with a limp, and several children. Dierdre stood there bravely, not budging until she ushered them all down, one at a time, while the Pandesians, over the mound of rubble, were closing in.

"Hurry!" Dierdre called to the stragglers, tightening her grip on a spear.

She soon realized that she wouldn't make it back down in time. She raised her spear, as did Marco beside her, and they turned to face off against the soldiers as the last of the people descended.

Three soldiers met them at once, and Dierdre ducked as one lunged for her; she then swung around and sliced his throat. Marco didn't wait, but ran forward and stabbed one through the heart. And when the third lunged for Marco's back, Dierdre rushed forward with a scream and jammed her spear in his back. The soldier spun around, and Marco stabbed him in the throat, felling him.

Dierdre heard a clamor, looked up, and saw dozens more soldiers appearing at the top of the mound.

"Let's go!" Marco urged.

They descended, rushing down the ladder as the Pandesians charged. Marco reached up and with a second to go, slammed closed the hatch and bolted it. There came the stomping of boots on the iron grate, as the Pandesians desperately tried to get in.

But there was no way, even for them. The iron was a foot thick, and their swords could not penetrate it.

Standing at the foot of the ladder, safely below, breathing hard, Dierdre looked at the group of citizens, then to Marco. He looked back, as disbelieving as she.

Somehow, they had done it.

*

Dierdre and Marco lingered with the dozens of people in a cavernous room below ground, all of them finally safe. They were cold, tired, shivering, and some of the children were crying. Dierdre wondered how long they could all survive down here. But at least, she told herself, she had saved them from an imminent, violent death, had given them more time, a

60

second chance at life, however long that was. She felt good about it. It helped her take her mind off her father, off all the devastation around her.

Dierdre paced, as she had for hours, wondering what to do next as she heard the entire city being destroyed above her. They could not stay down here forever, she knew that. Death was coming for them all.

The more she paced, the more a burning resolve began to grow within her. She thought of her dead father up there, of the sacrifices he had made, and she knew she had to follow in his footsteps. It was the only way to honor his legacy. Her thoughts turned to Alec and she remembered the work he had done, forging those chains, those spikes and slowly, an idea dawned on her.

Dierdre turned to Marco as she heard the cannon fire subside, who sat there, dejected, head in his hands.

"They've finished the first assault," she remarked. "That means their ships will be entering the canals soon."

He looked back at her, wondering.

"Let's not make it easy on them," she added.

He stared back, and slowly recognition dawned across his face.

"The chains?" he asked.

She nodded.

"Are they in the canals?" she asked, wondering if their work was completed before the invasion.

Marco nodded back with an expression of deadly seriousness.

"Alongside the harbor," he replied. "But not affixed. We did not have time before the invasion."

Dierdre nodded, feeling a sense of resolve.

"Then let's not wait another minute," she said, finally stopping pacing, filled with a sense of certainty.

Marco stood, too, a fresh look of determination in his eyes.

"You're mad," said an old man, overhearing, standing and coming up beside them, his voice filled with concern. "You'll get yourself killed!"

"The Pandesians are already here," said another. "Nothing can stop them. What's the point of destroying a few ships?"

"If we block the canals," Dierdre replied, "it will kill hundreds of soldiers. It will clog the canals."

"So?" asked another. "Will that stop the million behind them?"

"The city is already destroyed," another added. "Why bother?"

"Why?" Dierdre echoed, indignant. "Because it is what we do. It is who we are. It is what my father would have done."

"What is the alternative?" Marco added. "To stay down here and wait for our deaths?"

"At least down here you are safe," added another.

"I don't want to be safe," Dierdre replied. "I want to defend our city."

Some people shook their heads, while others looked away, fear and cowardice in their eyes.

"We will not risk our lives up there," one man with a withered arm finally said.

"I don't ask you to," Dierdre replied, cold and hard, not expecting anything from anyone. She was beyond that now. "I shall do it myself."

Dierdre began to walk toward one of the ladders, when she felt a hand on her arm. She turned to see Marco's serious brown eyes staring back at her.

"I will join you," he said.

Dierdre was touched.

Before she ascended, she turned and faced the crowd of scared, huddled faces, looking over each one. They seemed terrified, and she understood.

"Anyone else?" she asked, wanting to give them one last chance to join her.

But they all looked away in fear and shame.

"You'll be climbing to your death up there," one woman called out.

Dierdre nodded back.

"I don't doubt that," she replied.

Dierdre turned and began to ascend the ladder, one rung at a time, Marco behind her. It was a long climb in the blackness, her hands trembling from fear. Yet she forced herself to suppress her fears, to rise above them.

When they finally reached the top, they paused and looked at each other. Marco raised an eyebrow, as if asking if she were sure she wanted to do this. She nodded back silently, and they understood each other.

They reached out and, together, they pulled back the bolts. They gave the heavy iron slab one big push, and a moment later they were flooded with sunlight.

Ur.

Their   destiny   awaited   them.

CHAPTER FIFTEEN

Kyra rode across the countryside of Escalon, Andor thundering beneath her, Leo at her heels, the three of them cutting through the brush, breaking branches, rustling leaves, winding in and out of forest trails as they had been for hours. Ever since leaving Alva's side, Kyra felt a new sense of determination, of purpose, as she headed for her mother's original home, the source of her power, the place where all was supposed to be revealed.

The Lost Temple.

Her mind raced as she imagined it, each step increasing her sense of anticipation. It was there, Alva promised, that Kyra would find the clues she needed to lead her to her mother, and to find her own source of power. Kyra's heart pounded in anticipation. All her life she had wondered about her mother; she had wanted nothing more than to meet her, to hear her voice, to embrace her, to see if she was like her. She wanted so desperately to know if her mother was proud of her, to hear it in her mother's own words. That would make all of it, all these years of not knowing her, of not being raised by her, worth it.

Even more, Kyra longed to know where she had come from, who her real people were, who she was herself. Alva's words echoed in her mind. *The ancient ones. The original people. Protectors of Escalon. Those who kept the dragons at bay.* Kyra was proud to hail from such a lineage, and yet she wondered what it meant. It was a different race he was speaking of. A race of immortals, of all-powerful beings. How had they disappeared? Who had vanquished them? Had they truly disappeared at all?

Kyra sensed her mother was not entirely human, was more powerful than all the human race, yet she did not know how long ago she had lived, how much of that power had filtered down to her. Did she carry the same power her mother had? Or was Kyra of a mixed race? Was her mother immortal? Did that mean that Kyra was immortal, too?

Kyra rode and rode, realizing how lucky she was to be alive, and her thoughts drifted to Kyle. He had left so abruptly, returning to the tower, and her heart quickened as she knew he was heading into danger. What if she never saw him again? She did not completely understand her feelings for him, or why she cared so much. And that all made her feel out of control—and she did not like feeling out of control.

Kyra rode and rode, heading invariably south, until finally, as the sun grew long, she came upon a massive fork in the forest trail. A crude wooden sign pointed two ways, one to the west, toward the coast, in the direction, she knew, of the Sorrow, of the Lost Temple. And the other pointed east, with a sign that read ANDROS.

Her heart skipped a beat. *Andros*. She immediately thought of her father, of his being held captive. Kyra sat there, atop Andor, breathing hard, staring at the sign. It was like staring at her destiny. She wanted to go to both places at once.

But she knew she could not. She could only choose one fork, one place. And whichever route she chose, she knew, would have consequences for the rest of her life. She knew what she was supposed to do: she should follow Alva's orders and fork west, toward the temple, toward her mother. She had to find the source of her power, become a greater warrior, and survive for the sake of her father. And she had to find the clues that led her closer to her mother, to herself.

Yet, try as she did, Kyra had always led with her heart, not her mind. And as she sat there, atop Andor, breathing hard, her heart told her she could never leave her father rotting in prison. Not now, not ever. If he wasn't dead already, surely he would soon be executed. And if she turned away from him, his blood would be on her hands. That just wasn't who she was.

So, despite the sense of foreboding brewing within her, Kyra turned Andor east, away from the coastline, away from the Temple—and for Andros. Even as she was doing it, Kyra knew it was foolhardy. She knew she could not take on the Pandesian army, guarding Andros, by herself. She knew her father might already be dead. And she knew she was turning her back on her mother, her destiny, her mission.

Yet she had no choice. The wind in her hair, she already rode, charging toward Andros, toward her father.

"Father," she said, "wait for me."

CHAPTER SIXTEEN

Merk and Kyle hiked quickly through the forest of Ur as they had been for days, Merk wondering about this boy beside him. They had journeyed together in silence for days, and he realized he knew next to nothing about Kyle. He knew he had Kyle to thank for being alive, and it was a strange feeling; Merk had always looked out for himself and had never felt beholden to anyone. He had certainly never expected it from him, of all people. After all, Kyle was a Watcher, the most mysterious of them all, and had always been aloof.

Merk wondered if Kyle liked him at all, and was even more baffled that he had come back to save him. Fate had put them on this journey together, both with a shared mission to reach the Tower of Kos and protect the Sword of Fire. Yet if it weren't for that, Merk wondered if Kyle would have come back for him.

"Why did you save me?" Merk finally asked, needing, after all these days, to break the monotony, and the silence.

A long silence followed, one so long that Merk was sure Kyle did not hear him. Perhaps he would choose not to respond.

And then, hours later, when he least expected it, Kyle replied:

"Why wouldn't I?"

Merk looked over in surprise. Kyle's grey eyes seemed ancient, despite his young age.

"You came back for me," Merk said, "to spare my life before the trolls could end it."

"I did not come back for you," Kyle corrected. "I returned for the tower, to defend it."

"And yet you saved me."

Kyle shrugged.

"You were there. The tower was lost," Kyle replied.

Merk was starting to feel that Kyle didn't care about him at all.

"How did you know it was lost?" Merk asked.

"I just knew," Kyle replied, glum. "We must now help the kingdom where help is needed most. There is another tower, after all."

Merk wondered.

"When did you know the Sword was not there?" he asked, curious.

Kyle looked at him skeptically, as if debating whether to respond.

"I have always known," he finally admitted. "For centuries."

Merk was shocked.

"Yet you remained there," Merk said, slowly realizing. "For centuries, you stood guard there. At an empty tower. For an empty mission...." Merk was flabbergasted. "Why?"

Kyle cleared his throat.

"It was no empty mission," he retorted. "One tower holds the Sword, one does not. And yet they each hold it in their own way, each has their role to play. One cannot serve as a decoy without the other. Both must be equally well guarded. If only one was guarded, the enemy would know where to concentrate their attack."

Merk pondered that.

"And yet now," Merk replied, "with the Tower of Ur destroyed, everyone will know. Your precious secret, after all these centuries, is lost."

Kyle sighed.

"True," he replied. "Yet if we reach Kos first, we can warn them. They can take precautions."

"And you think their precautions will really hold back the entire nation of Marda?" Merk pressed. "Or the Pandesian army? The Tower of Kos will fall, too, sooner or later. The Sword will be lost. The Flames will lower. All of Marda will pour in—and Escalon will be lost. It will be a plundered land. A wasteland."

Kyle sighed. He fell silent for a long time.

"You still don't understand," Kyle said. "Escalon was never free. Not since the ancient ones died. Not since the first dragon appeared. And not since we lost The Staff of Truth."

"The Staff of Truth?" Merk asked, baffled.

But Kyle just stared ahead in silence, leaving Merk to wonder. He was endlessly cryptic, and it drove Merk crazy; questions only led to more questions, and half the time he spoke he referenced things which Merk would never understand.

They continued for hours more in silence, trekking through the forest, until finally there came a gushing noise; they emerged from the thick woods to find themselves facing a raging river. Merk was in awe at the sight of the white, foaming waters of the Tanis. There it flowed, its wall of rapids blocking their way, seeming impossible to cross. Yet there was no other way.

Merk knew he couldn't just stand here. He began to step forward toward the water, when he felt a firm hand on his chest. He looked at Kyle, puzzled.

"What is it?" he asked.

Kyle stared into the wood line. He didn't say a word—he didn't have to. Merk could tell he sensed something. The way of Watchers was a mystery.

Merk had great respect for his friend, and stopped, trusting him. He examined the landscape, the thick woods on the far side of the river, yet he saw nothing.

"I see nothing," he said. "Perhaps you are being overly cautious."

66

After a long wait, Merk stepped forward, and Kyle walked beside him, the two entering the clearing and approaching the river's edge. Merk took a step, wondering if he could brave the rapids, and immediately, the freezing, strong currents nearly knocked him over.

Merk stumbled back to the safety of shore, realizing they would need some way to cross it. He saw some motion downriver, something bobbing, and he walked along the sand with Kyle until he spotted a small boat tied to a rock, rocking wildly in the currents, just big enough to hold them both.

"I don't like it," Kyle said, coming up beside him.

"You have another idea?" Merk asked.

Kyle examined the currents, and the horizon beyond it, but fell silent.

Merk stepped into the small canoe, nearly falling out as it rocked wildly, and as Kyle got in beside him, he reached over and sliced the rope with his dagger. The boat swayed violently. He pushed off with the oar, and a moment later, they were caught up in the currents, racing downriver.

Merk and Kyle rowed, struggling to cut across the raging waters, as whitecaps crashed all around them. As they fought their way their small boat nearly turned sideways; Merk felt certain it would capsize.

Kyle looked in all directions, as if expecting something to attack them, and that kept Merk on edge.

Finally, though, they were able to get out ahead of the current. They cut across the river, and they reached the other side, dripping wet from the spray.

They jumped out onto the shore, and no sooner had they set down when the currents took away the boat. Merk turned to watch it shoot downstream, soon lost in a sea of white.

Kyle stood there and studied the tree line with a concerned expression, still appearing troubled.

"What is it?" Merk asked again, feeling on edge himself. "Surely if there were something, then—"

No sooner had he finished uttering the words than he suddenly froze. There came a noise, sounding like a snarl crossed with a howl, one that made his hairs stand. It came from something evil.

Kyle, still watching, raised his staff.

"Baylors," he finally said, his voice ominous.

"What are—"

No sooner had Merk uttered the words when out of the tree line there appeared a pack of savage beasts, charging right for them. There were four of them, looking like rhinos, yet with six horns instead of one, and with thick black hides. They each had two long fangs, as sharp as swords, and intense white eyes, and they bore down on Kyle and Merk, the thunder of their hooves shaking the ground.

Merk turned and looked back at the gushing river, and realized they were trapped.

"We can swim," Merk said, realizing it might be better to take their chances in the rapids.

"So can they," Kyle replied.

Merk felt a cold dread climb up his back. The baylors closed in, now hardly twenty yards away, the sound thunderous, and Merk, not knowing what else to do, reached up with his dagger, took aim, and threw.

He watched it sail end over end, right for one of the beasts' eyes.

Merk anticipated it puncturing his eye, dropping it to the ground—but the baylor merely reached up with its paw and knocked it away like a toothpick, barely even slowing.

Merk swallowed. He had just given it the best he had.

"Get down!" Kyle shouted as the first bore down on them.

The beast lifted its razor-sharp claws to slice Merk in half, and Merk dropped to the ground, praying that Kyle knew what he was doing. He ducked under the shadow of the great beast's foot, about to crush him.

The beast went flying sideways, to Merk's immense relief, as Kyle struck it with his staff. A sharp cracking noise tore through the air as Kyle sent the beast flying, then rolling side over side, the ground shaking. Merk breathed a sigh of relief, realizing how close he had come to death.

Kyle swung his staff at another baylor as it approached; he struck it in the chest and it flew backwards, up in the air a good twenty feet, landing on its back, rolling and taking out another one with it. Merk looked over at Kyle in awe, shocked at his power, wondering what else he could do.

"This way!" Kyle ordered.

Kyle ran for the beast that was on its back, while the other bore down on them and other two began to recover. Merk joined him, running faster than he had ever run in his life. They reached the beast and Merk was shocked as Kyle jumped on its back. It writhed and stood. Merk knew this was crazy, but he didn't know what else to do, so he jumped on, too, grabbing onto the thick hide, slipping and clawing his way up for dear life as the baylor rose to its full height.

A moment later the baylor was bucking wildly, the two of them riding it. Merk, slipping, was certain he would die here. The other beasts charged right for them.

Then Kyle leaned down and whispered in the baylor's ear, and suddenly, to Merk's shock, it became still. It lifted its head, as if listening to Kyle, and as Kyle kicked it, the baylor shrieked, made a trumpeting sound like an elephant, and charged for its companions.

The other beasts were clearly not expecting this. They hardly knew what to do as their friend charged them. The first one could not react in time as the beast lowered its head and gored him in the side. The beast

68

shrieked, dropping to its side, and the beast they were riding trampled over it, killing it.

The beast then raised its horns and lifted upward, goring another one in the throat, and rising up until it dropped, gurgling, dead.

Their beast then ran like thunder, aiming for the final beast.

But the final beast, seeing what was happening, charged back, infuriated. When the beast they were riding lunged for it, the final beast ducked and swiped. The beast beneath them shrieked as its legs were cut out from under it.

Merk felt himself sliding and a moment later he tumbled and fell, Kyle with him, smashing into rock and dirt, and losing his breath as he tumbled, sure he was breaking his ribs.

He lay there on the ground and watched the final beast attack, watched Kyle stunned, winded, too, and he was sure he would be crushed to death.

But then, somehow, the beast they were riding managed to regain strength enough for one last blow—it turned, swiped, and sliced the final beast through the chest.

The final beast dropped to the ground, dead, while the beast they were riding buckled and fell. It let out a great snort, and then a moment later, it, too, lay dead, atop its friend.

Merk stood there, breathing hard, looking out at the four dead beasts, hardly able to process it. They had survived. Somehow, they had survived.

He turned and looked at Kyle, still in awe, and Kyle smiled back.

"That was the easy part," he said.

*

Kyle and Merk marched, trekking in the silence, crossing the great plains of Escalon, heading invariably south and east, heading, somewhere in the distance for the Devil's Finger, the ancient peninsula of Kos. They had been journeying for days, never stopping since their encounter with those baylors. Kyle tried to lose himself, to drown out his thoughts, in the landscape. Yet it was not easy to do. There flashed through his mind images of the Tower of Ur falling, of his fellow Watchers' deaths. He burned with indignation and felt a stronger desire than ever to reach Kos, secure the Sword before Marda could arrive, and ensure Escalon's survival.

Despite everything, Kyle had taken a liking to this human, his new traveling companion, Merk. He had displayed bravery in battle, in defending the tower, even when he had not needed to. There were very few humans whom Kyle liked, but this one, for some reason, he did. Kyle could sense in him, deep down, a struggle to change, to cast off his old life—and it was something Kyle could relate to. Kyle knew he could trust him and that he would make a fine brother-in-arms, even if he were not of his race.

Kyle studied the horizon as the sun lowered in the sky, contemplating the best way to approach the barren and inhospitable peninsula of the Devil's Finger. In the distance he could already begin to see the icy peaks of Kos, the mountain range seeming to reach the sky, and he knew a formidable journey lay ahead of them. His mind swam with thoughts of the tower, the trolls—of Kyra—and he tried to push them away, to stay focused on his mission.

And yet as he was hiking, immersed in his thoughts, halfway across the great plains, something inside Kyle made him suddenly stop. He stood there, frozen, listening to something on the wind.

Merk stopped beside him, looking at him questioningly. It was the first time they had stopped in days.

Kyle turned and surveyed the plains before him. He turned slowly in the opposite direction and looked due south. As he did, he felt a pulse of energy course through his body, and he knew. Life and death was at stake. He was needed.

"What is it?" Merk asked.

Kyle stood there, silent for many minutes. He closed his eyes, listening to the wind, trying to understand.

And then, suddenly, like a spear in his back, he knew. Kyra. She was in grave danger; he felt it in every bone in his body.

He turned to Merk.

"I cannot continue with you," he said, barely believing his own words.

Merk stared back, clearly shocked.

"What do you mean?" he asked.

"Kyra," he said, still trying to understand what it was. "She needs me."

Merk frowned, but Kyle reached out and clasped Merk's arm and looked him in the eyes with all intensity.

"Continue without me," Kyle told him. "When you reach Kos, secure the Sword. Do whatever you have to. I will catch up."

Merk looked disappointed, clearly not understanding. Kyle wished he could explain, but how could he explain his love for Kyra? How could he explain that it was more important to him even than the fate of Escalon?

Without another word, Kyle, burning with urgency, turned and raced south, faster than he'd ever run, skipping across the plains, knowing he would save Kyra or die trying.

CHAPTER SEVENTEEN

His Glorious Ra, Most Holy and Supreme Leader of Pandesia, stood atop the battlements of Andros and looked out over the countryside of Escalon, taking it all in. It was now his. All of it. He grinned in satisfaction.

There, in the distance, he could see his armies charging north, pursuing the trolls, hacking them to death as they fled. It had been a rout. The nation of Marda was no doubt a vicious one, the trolls twice the size of his men, their strength legendary, and their leader, Vesuvius, high on the list of those that Ra wanted to capture and torture personally. And yet, still, he had prevailed. He had lost thousands of men fighting them—but he had merely sent in thousands more. It was the great convenience of having a slave army, gathered from all corners of the Empire. His people were dispensable.

Eventually, as Ra knew they would, the trolls buckled under his waves of manpower, realizing, as most conquered nations eventually do, that they were useless against his great might. Ra was, after all, invincible. He had never lost, and he never would. It had been written in the stars. He was the Great One, the One Who Had Never Been Touched, and the One Who Could Not Die.

As Ra watched his forces spread north throughout the countryside, radiating in all directions, he realized he had been way too kind with Escalon. He had foolishly thought they would go the way of all his other conquered territories, would submit to the rule of his royal governors. He had given them too many liberties—and now it was time to change all that. Now it was time for them to learn who he was. Now it was time to make them suffer.

This petty war with Escalon had been a distraction for the Great and Awesome Ra, a nuisance that had diverted him from other pressing duties, from other wars. He would make these people of Escalon pay the price. This time, he would enslave the entire nation. He would cover every last inch of Escalon with soldiers, would murder all the men, torture all the women, put the children in labor camps, and leave his mark on every inch of this land. It would be unrecognizable when he was done. They would become an example for all nations that dared defy him.

Ra had been foolish to listen to his advisors, to listen to the people who boasted of the great warriors of Escalon, how independent they were, and the best way to rule them. He should have trusted his own instincts and done what he always did: crush everyone. Raze their towns. Leave them with nothing. After all, people who no longer existed could hardly defy you.

In the distance Ra could hear the reassuring sound of his cannons, booming somewhere on the horizon as his fleets attacked Ur. His armies and fleets were attacking Escalon from all sides and there would be no escape. Soon, any pockets of resistance would be wiped out. The leader of the resistance, the man they called Duncan, was already in the dungeon, and Ra looked forward to visiting him, to crushing the last of the last free spirits.

As he watched the trolls flee, Ra already knew where they were heading. Southeast. The Devil's Finger, the Tower of Kos. They were after the Sword of Fire, were desperate to lower the Flames, to open the gates for the nation of Marda. How predictable. Did they not know the Great and Awesome Ra would never allow this? Indeed, his forces were already in motion, preparing to destroy all these trolls before they could cause any more trouble for him.

"A beautiful sight, isn't it?" came a voice.

Ra turned and his smile fell as he saw Enis stepping up beside him, the boy who thought he was King. There he stood, resembling his father, the man he had sold out and killed. Ra fumed. The arrogance, to think he could stand this close to The Great and Holy Ra.

"It is a sight I never expected to see," Enis continued. "Marda always threatened Escalon. And yet now they are fleeing from us."

"Us?" Ra asked, looking down at him with disdain, fury rising within him. This arrogant, presumptuous boy clearly had no idea that *no one* ever approached Ra without kneeling and bowing his head to the ground—and that no one *ever* spoke to Ra until Ra had spoken first.

Yet there he stood, smiling back with his stupidity and arrogance.

"Escalon will be entirely under our rule soon enough," Enis continued, "and my people will do exactly as we wish."

"*We?*" Ra asked, standing taller with pride and indignation.

Enis looked back, equally proud and arrogant.

"I am King now, after all," Enis replied, as if it were obvious. "I handed you your greatest victory, a victory that did not even cost you a soldier, thanks to me. I delivered my father, too, along with Duncan and all the great warriors. You have plenty to thank me for."

Ra had never felt such disgust in his life, and deep inside he could feel himself about to blow. It was all he could do to keep himself from reaching out and strangling the boy.

Adding insult to injury, Enis reached up and actually dared to lay a hand on Ra's shoulder.

"You need me," Enis continued, still not realizing the danger he was in. "These are my people. I know how to rule them. Without me, you have nothing."

Ra took a deep breath, then spoke with a voice trembling with anger.

72

"Do you know how many kings I have instilled and deposed?" Ra asked in his deep, rumbling voice. "How many lands, how many nations, have been my plaything? And yet the kings, *my* kings, all think the same thing: they imagine that *they* have power. That it is *their* land. *Their* people. How quickly delusions grow. There is one thing that they always seem to forget."

Ra reached up and with a quick and sudden motion, grabbed Enis by the back of his shirt, took several steps forward, dragging him, and with a great cry hurled him over the edge of the parapets.

Enis shrieked as he flailed and fell through the air. Finally, he landed with a splat, face first on the stone far below.

Ra looked down, smiled, and took a deep breath. He was starting to feel better now, seeing that insolent boy's mangled body so far below.

"Power," Ra said down to the dead body, "is illusory."

*

Bant strode down the capital streets, feeling a sense of euphoria, of the power to come lying just out of his grasp. He had not been this giddy since he was a boy. The capital was safely in the hands of the Pandesians now. The coup he had helped orchestrate had worked. The old King Tarnis was dead, Duncan was imprisoned, and Enis, the boy he had helped rise to power, sat as the new King.

Bant grinned widely. Enis owed him his title, his kingship, and with Pandesia ruling Escalon and Enis their instilled ruler, that meant that Bant would have unlimited power. With Enis in power, he and his people were untouchable. Pandesia could never harm him, never invade his canyon, his stronghold, and he had assured his and his people's safety for years to come. More than that, he had assured their power in the new Escalon. With all the other strongholds invaded, Barris would be the last and only remaining bastion of freedom, of independence.

Soon enough, Escalon would look to him to lead. And he would kill Enis when he least expected it, and naturally rise to power.

Bant grinned wide, turning through a city gate, rushing to see Enis right now. He had gambled on the right side, indeed. He could only imagine if he had put his lot with Duncan, where he would be right now. Dead, by a Pandesian blade.

Sure, he had had to betray some of his people, Duncan most of all. But that barely bothered him. A conscience, he learned long ago, was something he had to let go of if he was determined to rise to power. And determined he was. One of the things he looked forward to the most, in fact, was watching Duncan hang from the gallows. Only then would he feel completely at ease.

Bant turned the corner, finally reaching the palace entrance, and he looked up in the early morning sun. He raised a hand to his eyes and could see, high up, there Enis stood, beside the battlements, Ra by his side. Bant grinned. The two of them were alone up there. That meant that, already, Ra was turning to Enis for council. Enis would be untouchable, and Bant would be, too.

Bant was about to rush to the stairs, ascend to speak to Enis, when suddenly he thought he detected motion out of the corner of his eye. He looked up, and for a moment he could not process what he saw. There was Enis. But he was no longer standing on the parapets. Instead, he was shrieking, falling, flying through the air.

Bant watched in horror as he hit the ground with a splat, but feet away from him. Dead.

He looked up, wondering if Enis had slipped. But he saw Ra looking down, grinning, and he knew he had not. Bant could not believe it. Enis was dead. And Ra had killed him.

Bant gulped. His hope for power, for safety, was already crushed. Already, Pandesia had gone back on their word. He, too, had been betrayed. No one was safe.

Bant jumped into the shadows, hoping Ra had not seen him. He stood there, his back to the wall, sweating, breathing hard.

Then, when enough time had passed, he darted from the shadows and ran. He ran and ran, out the gate, away from the capital, and somewhere into the day, determined to get as far away from the capital as he could.

CHAPTER EIGHTEEN

Kyra rode across Escalon, as she had all day and night, desperate to reach Andros, to free her father before it was too late. It had been a long, harrowing night of riding, guided only by the stars, and yet she had persevered, knowing every moment was precious, knowing there was no chance to stop.

Despite the sleepless night, Kyra felt stronger than ever. She rode, driven by a sense of purpose, and felt ready, ever since her healing, to take on the hordes of the world. She reflected on her training, her newfound ability to summon her powers, to move objects with just with her mind, and she knew they were real. She felt ready to confront whatever army faced her, to do whatever she had to do to save her father—even if it meant her own death. She only prayed that it was not too late.

As she emerged from the woods and crested a series of hills, finally the night sky gave way to a breaking dawn, and all of Escalon opened up before her. She looked out through the early morning mist, the countryside sparkling in the dawn, and her heart fluttered in anticipation as she finally spotted, on the horizon, the contours of the great capital of Andros, sprawling, it seemed, to the end of the world. Here was the city she remembered from her youth, with its massive, arched drawbridge, its imposing stone gates, its gatehouses, battlements, turrets, and imposing façade. Her heart beat faster. Her father, she knew, was behind those walls, and this time, nothing of this earth would stop her from getting him back.

Kyra kicked Andor and they rode even faster, heading for the city. She saw in the distance the garrison of Pandesian soldiers stationed before the city, a sea of yellow and blue, glistening in the dawn, and she tensed, prepared.

As she neared, they clearly noticed her approach; a horn sounded, and hundreds of troops broke off and began charging right for her, lances lowered, visors down.

Kyra tightened her grip on her staff, increasing her speed, ready for anything. Those soldiers stood between her and the gates, and that, she could not allow. Kyra let out a battle cry, knowing this charge was reckless, yet knowing she had no choice. She was stronger now, she could feel it; she had powers from her training, powers she had never had before. She felt she could fight this army.

Kyra charged, closing the gap as hundreds of Pandesians in their clanging armor rushed forward in rows to meet her. She would not shy away, but meet them fearlessly. She could see them all grinning, as if expecting a quick and easy victory—and she was determined to give them a different outcome.

As the first sword came down for her head, Kyra focused on her innate power. She felt an intense heat rise up within her, tingling in her arms, hands. She felt more alive than ever, and she swung her staff and knocked swords from three soldiers' hands in one blow. She swung around again and slashed two more soldiers across the chest, knocking them off their horses. She felt a foreign, unknown power coursing through her, hinted at in her training with Alva, one that had always been just out of her reach. She felt, oddly, as if her mother were with her.

Kyra ducked as one soldier swung a flail at her head, then she cracked him in the ribs, felling him. She never slowed, charging forward into the thick of battle, slashing and jabbing soldiers every which way, dodging and ducking and weaving, feeling her supernatural power urge her forward, making her faster than all those around her as she cut a path through the ranks. She kept in her sights the contours of Andros, and kept in the forefront of her mind her father, imprisoned, needing her help—and she let her adrenaline push her on.

Leo and Andor fought as they went, too, Andor kicking viciously, knocking out other horses, felling their riders, Leo snarling and biting, killing any soldier who came too close to her. Kyra swung her staff again and again, and as she did, she began to close her eyes, finding she could tune in better that way. She summoned her power and was able to summon a yellow orb of light, shooting forth from the end of the staff, and she killed a dozen soldiers in a single explosion.

Kyra swung again the staff again, and as she did, an orb flew in the other direction, taking out a dozen more soldiers.

She swung again—and again. Soon the battlefield was filled with dead soldiers, hundreds of them lying on the ground all around her. It was as if she were a tornado, cutting through their ranks.

Kyra continued to charge, getting ever closer to the bridge to Andros. She had to cross it. She swung her staff as she went, feeling invincible, shooting orbs of light in every direction and felling dozens of soldiers. She took aim and blew up the stone garrison, killing hundreds more Pandesian soldiers as they tried to exit, thinking of her father as she took vengeance for him.

As Kyra approached the bridge, she saw the portcullis beyond it open, and she watched as thousands more soldiers came charging out of the city, right for her. It was a sea of blue and yellow.

She swung her staff again, but this time, to her horror, no orb appeared. Somehow, her power had stopped—there was now nothing in her hand but an ordinary staff. Had Alva been right? Was she not ready yet?

Having felt so invincible but moments before, Kyra now looked out at the sight before her and felt more vulnerable than ever. She realized now that she was in grave danger. She looked out, struggling to understand what had happened, and as she did, she spotted a single dark sorcerer, wearing a scarlet cape, emerging from the city. She saw the red orb of light in his hand, and she sensed immediately that she was up against a power far greater than hers.

Suddenly, Kyra felt the first blow; a soldier charged and struck her on the shoulder with his shield. Knocked off her horse, she landed on the ground, winded, tumbling amidst the hostile army.

Kyra raised her staff and did her best to block the blows as the Pandesian soldiers closed in on her. She swung left and right, the clang of her staff ringing out as she blocked one sword slash after the next. They struck her with swords and halberds and flails, and she managed to turn in every direction and duck and weave and block all the attacks. She even managed to strike back, killing many and knocking several down.

Andor and Leo rushed forward and helped, Andor viciously kicking soldiers back, biting them, tearing them to pieces, while Leo leapt and sank his fangs into the arms of anyone who came too close to her.

Yet as more and more soldiers closed in, their ranks never-ending, Kyra felt herself tiring. She lowered her shoulders just a bit, slowing down, and one blow snuck through, wounding her shoulder, making her cry out. At the same time, a new group of soldiers surrounded Andor and Leo, clubbing them until they were on their backs, pounced upon from all sides.

Kyra felt horrific pain in her other shoulder as another blow snuck through, this one from a war hammer. Then a moment later, she felt herself kicked in the chest, and went stumbling back. There were just too many of them, and she realized with horror that she was too exhausted, too weak to stop them all. Alva had been right; she did not have the strength to take on this army alone. She had managed to kill hundreds of soldiers, to fight brilliantly, and to summon her powers to make it happen. But that dark sorcerer had overpowered her somehow, had stopped up the source of her powers, and she knew, with her human energy waning, her time was over.

Kyra felt the blows descending upon her from all directions now, and after a particularly vicious blow of a club to her ribcage, she stumbled and fell to the ground.

She lay there, hardly able to breathe, the blows still coming, unable to move. She looked up as the sky blackened with men, and saw them all closing in on her, raising their weapons. She reached for her staff, but it was kicked away from her. Another soldier stepped on her wrist with his boot. She lay there, helpless, looking up at what she could see of the sky, and knew she was about to die.

A Pandesian soldier stepped up, raised his sword high with both hands, and stared down at her. She could see the hatred in his eyes. He was preparing to finish her off, and she had no doubt that he would.

She closed her eyes and braced herself. She no longer felt fear; just remorse. She wished, more than anything, she had been able to free her father before she died.

I am sorry, Father, she thought. *I let you down.*

CHAPTER NINETEEN

Alec stood at the bow of the ship and stared out into the eerie harbor before them. He watched, transfixed, as they sailed between outcroppings of rock, weaving their way circuitously through the archipelago of the Lost Isles. They passed one abandoned isle after the next, all covered in a shroud of fog and mist. The silence was punctuated only by the sound of exotic creatures leaping from the water and splashing in the mist; Alec rarely caught a glimpse of them, leaving him to wonder just what else was swimming beneath the surface. It only deepened his sense of mystery of this place.

These islands seemed so desolate here at the end of the world, separated from the mainland by thousands of miles of ocean, hidden by a persistent mist. Alec watched in fascination as they passed enormous blue boulders, emerging from the sea like hands reaching for the sky. They passed islands made entirely of seaweed, immense black birds cawing on them, as large as he, watching him pass as if he were trespassing in their land. They passed isles of jagged rock, the terrain so sharp there was nowhere to even set foot. He had seen nothing even remotely inhabitable.

A breeze picked up and they turned into a narrow channel, and there came a new, distinct noise below. Alec looked down to see long, blue sea grass rising up from the waters and clinging to the hull. The ship slowed, and he looked out, concerned.

"We're stuck!" he said.

But Sovos, to his surprise, merely shook his head and continued looking straight ahead, unperturbed.

"Illuvian Sea Grass," he said calmly. "As ancient as these islands. It's our welcome. They're guiding us into the isles."

Alec watched in fascination as the tentacles latched onto the ship, winding their way up the hull. As they did they made a little popping noise, and the sea of grass began to sway, as if it were alive. The air was soon filled with the sound of a thousand faint popping noises, the sound of grass sucking and clinging to the ship, pulling them forward. The ocean appeared to be throbbing.

Alec finally saw the looming land mass before them, increasingly revealed as the mist began to lift, and the closer they came, the more Alec felt a weird sensation. It was as if something in the air were enveloping him. They sailed into a warm fog, and he felt as if he were breathing in moisture. It made him sleepy, relaxed. The Lost Isles, he was beginning to realize, were unlike any place he'd ever been.

"Who do the isles belong to?" Alec asked, as they wound their way deeper into the islands.

79

"No one," Sovos replied.

Alec was puzzled.

"Are they not part of Escalon?" he asked. "Or Marda? Or Pandesia?"

Sovos shook his head.

"They are a nation unto themselves. They are their own people. Yet they are more than just a nation."

As Alec struggled to understand, the thick fog finally lifted and it took his breath away as, before him, he saw the most spectacular landscape he had ever seen. There was a large island, sparkling in the mist, with a silver hue in the light. The sun seemed to shine down just on this place, making it look positively magical. Waves crashed into soaring cliffs, and high above, the island was filled with verdant fields and rolling hills of grass, yet also, inexplicably, dotted with peaks of ice, despite the warm breezes rolling off the ocean. None of it made any sense. The island was ringed by a beach of silver sand. It was like landing in heaven.

Even more strange, Alec could see a crowd of people had gathered on the beach, as if awaiting them. They stood there silently, several hundred islanders, dressed in silver robes, with long silver hair and silver eyes, and silver swords on their belts. They stared out at Alec, and as he met their eyes, the strangest thing happened: he felt an immediate connection with them. It was as if he had come home. It was the strangest feeling. His entire life, Alec had never felt at home, not in his village, and not really with anyone in his family. He had always felt like an outcast, like he didn't truly belong. But here, with these people, he felt, oddly, that he was amongst his people.

As their boat touched shore, pulled gently to the sand by the sea grass, Sovos jumped down from the ship onto the beach, and walked right for the people as if he belonged here. Alec followed, jumping down as well, his feet sinking softly in the sand, cushioning his fall. After so many days at sea, it felt strange to be on dry land again.

Alec walked forward with Sovos, and all the islanders stood there, silent, watching him carefully. He could feel all the eyes on him. His path was blocked by a middle-aged man with a stern expression, a head taller than the others, who stood before him, expressionless. He stared at Alec, intense, neither hostile nor welcoming.

"We have been awaiting you," he said, his voice dark, other-worldly. "For too many years."

Alec saw all the others staring at him with equal intensity, as if he were their messiah, and he was baffled.

"But...I don't know you," he replied.

Even as he uttered the words, Alec felt they were untrue. Somehow he knew all of these people.

"Don't you?" the man asked.

The man suddenly turned and walked, his feet crunching on the silver sand, into the landscape, and all the others watched Alec, as if expecting him to follow.

Alec looked over at Sovos, who nodded back in affirmation.

Alec took a step, following the man, and the others fell in behind him.

As he walked, leaving the beach, entering grass, Alec looked out and surveyed the island before him. It was breathtaking. He walked through bountiful farms framed by abundant trees, bearing fruits of all shapes and sizes and colors, unlike anything he had ever seen. Rolling green hills stretched to the horizon, the entire island filled with goodness and bounty. Honey flowed from ancient, twisted trees, and schools of fish leapt in the lakes.

Alec was burning with curiosity as he caught up to their leader. They continued to walk in silence, twisting and turning through the exotic landscape. Finally, they turned a bend, and on the other side of a series of hills, Alec saw what could only be their main village. It was made up of simple dwellings, cottages built of shining, silver granite, each one sparkling, as if made of diamonds. In the center was a large, triangular building, looking like a temple.

The man stopped and turned to Alec.

"The home of the Sword," he said cryptically.

As Alec stared back, wondering, all the villagers emerged from their dwellings and a large crowd surrounded him.

The man turned to Alec.

"Welcome home," he said.

Alec shook his head, confused, overwhelmed.

"I am from Soli," he replied, trying to think it through. "I am not from here."

The man shook his head.

"You don't even know," he said, mysteriously.

Before Alec could ask what he meant, the man led him forward, to the triangular building. Its silver door opened slowly as they neared.

Alec walked inside the dim dwelling and stopped, stunned. The room, with its high, pointed ceiling, no windows, and shining silver walls, was completely barren—save for one, singular object. In its center sat an anvil made of silver.

And on that anvil, a sword.

An unfinished sword.

Alec, mesmerized by the weapon, found himself walking forward as if drawn by a magnet, unable to look anywhere else.

He stopped beside it, and slowly reached out with shaking hands. There was a tremendous energy coming off of it, a vibration which shook the very air.

Alec touched the sword, and felt a bolt of energy course through his wrist, his arm. He lifted it ever so slowly, this half-forged sword, and felt it vibrating in his hand. It was the strangest thing, but holding this sword, for the first time in his life, he felt what it meant to be truly alive. He felt as if he were meant to be here—as if his whole life had been lived for this moment.

Alec turned, holding it—and he saw all the people inside, all looking back at him, a look of hope and expectation in their eyes.

"The unfinished sword," their leader said. "Without it, Escalon is lost."

Alec felt it humming within him, and he felt his life's purpose in his hands. The smith within him was taking over.

"This is why we need you, Alec," Sovos explained. "It is *you*. You and you alone can finish forging it."

Alec looked back, stunned.

"But why me?" he asked.

"Because you are one of us, Alec, and Escalon needs you."

He stepped forward and stared down, eyes shining with intensity.

"Don't let us down, Alec."

CHAPTER TWENTY

Anvin marched through the wasteland, dragging one foot before the other in the baking heat of the desert, every step an effort, each step making him more certain that he would die out here. The blood from his wounds had dried long ago and it was caked to his skin, mixing with the dirt, each step making him feel as if his wounds were reopening. Still covered in welts and bruises, in agony from being trampled, his body swollen with heat and wounds, each step required a Herculean effort. He felt as if he were walking underwater.

Anvin forced himself to look up, needing a reason to go on, and as he did, he spotted in the distance a sight that made his heart beat faster. There, on the horizon, was the tail end of the Pandesian army, marching away from him, heading north, leaving a trail of destruction in its wake. The army shimmered, a sea of yellow and gold, moving forward like a giant worm through his homeland, destroying one village at a time.

Now, finally, it had slowed, its million men unable to rush through the bottleneck of the mountains. Anvin had his chance to catch up to it. He was approaching the rear lines, the stragglers, the hangers-on, the ones Pandesia didn't really care about. They relegated them here because they had no reason to watch their backs. They owned all of Escalon now—or so they thought.

The army moved so slow that it barely moved at all, and Anvin, despite his wounds, closed in on them. He had to reach them before they reached the cliffs of Everfall, a path impossible for him to climb in his condition. He fixed his eye on a few soldiers at the end of the line, stragglers, men who had clearly been enslaved. He spotted some who were lame, some boys, and some old men. Any would make easy targets.

What he needed was the perfect match; he needed to find a soldier just his size, whose armor he could pilfer. And a soldier with a Pandesian horse to ride. With that, he could make it past all the others, all the way to the capital. It was his only hope.

Yet Anvin's conscience would not allow him to strike an old man or young boy or anyone who was maimed. Instead, as he approached, he tried to find a target he could feel justified in attacking. Soon enough, he did.

In the very rear, closest to him, stood a Pandesian taskmaster. He was whipping the others, shouting harshly in a language Anvin could not understand, while boys and old men stumbled beneath his long whip. He would do perfectly.

Anvin increased his speed, moving as fast as he could, and he soon bore down on him. The one advantage he had was that no one bothered to look back, to check over their shoulder. Why would they, after all? They had just conquered a land. Who would expect an attack from behind?

Anvin mustered all his remaining strength and felt a rush of adrenaline, enough to make him forget his pain for just a moment. He increased his pace, lifted his head a little higher, one eye still swollen shut, and set his sights on the taskmaster.

"ACHVOOT!" the taskmaster shrieked, as he whipped a young boy. The boy cried out and finally fell, while the taskmaster stepped up and flayed him again and again. All the others continued to move on, leaving the boy to his fate.

Anvin felt a rush of fury, seeing the boy being flayed to death. He drew his sword and, thinking of Durge, he used his last ounce of strength as he rushed forward with it. He ran, stumbling, gaining momentum as he went, and as he got near, he raised his sword and let out a guttural cry.

The taskmaster did not hear him at first, the sound of the whip dominating the air. At the last moment he turned and looked behind him and a startled look crossed his face as he saw Anvin attacking him from behind.

Anvin gave him no time to react. With his mouth still agape, Anvin lunged and ran his sword through his gut.

The taskmaster stood there for a moment, frozen in shock, then dropped dead to the ground.

Anvin stood there, breathing hard, exhausted from that small effort, amazed he still had enough left in him. He paid dearly for it, though, so exhausted that the world spun around him. Moments later, he collapsed.

*

Anvin woke to see a boy, bloody, tapping his face, staring down with concern. Anvin woke, realizing immediately, as he saw the slash marks across the boy's face, blood dripping from them, that it was the boy that the taskmaster had whipped.

Anvin looked over and saw the dead taskmaster lying beside him, and it all came rushing back.

The boy extended a hand and Anvin took it, allowing him to pull him back to his feet.

"I owe you my life," the boy said. He had a look of terror across his face. "They enslaved my entire family, I'm the only one who is left. Please," he repeated, "please don't turn me in to them. They will kill me."

Anvin turned and looked out at the army, about a hundred yards ahead on the horizon, and he knew that allowing this boy to survive, this witness to his crime, would jeopardize his life. He knew it was the prudent thing to do.

84

Yet he would never harm the boy, prudent or not. That was not who he was.

Anvin looked down at the taskmaster's corpse. Luckily, he was his size.

"Can you help me?" Anvin asked, his throat parched, gesturing to the body.

The boy looked back and forth from Anvin to the corpse, and finally, recognition dawned.

He rushed forward and began to strip the dead soldier of his armor. Anvin watched the boy, with his olive skin, curly hair, and intelligent green eyes, perhaps thirteen, and he admired his energy, his enthusiasm, despite his wounds. He needed him, he realized. Until he was back on his feet, he needed help.

The boy quickly stripped the soldier of his armor and held it up to Anvin, one piece at a time, making adjustments, making sure it was a good fit as he placed it on Anvin. Anvin felt himself getting heavier with each piece, felt his energy depleting as he sweated even more. Yet he knew he had to do this if he had any hope of reaching Andros.

Soon, he wore it all. One painstaking piece at a time. Out of breath, he felt as if he weighed a million pounds, sweating inside the metal suit. Yet he had done it. He knew he could make it now all the way to the capital. He felt he had a chance again.

Anvin heard a neighing, and he turned and was thrilled to see that the boy had brought over the taskmaster's horse. The boy helped him mount it, and as he sat there, he saw the boy standing there, looking up at him with hopeful eyes.

"I will die out here," the boy said. "They will kill me, the moment they find this man dead. Please, take me with you. Allow me to be your squire. I shall be faithful, always. My name is Septin."

Anvin sighed. He sat there, looking the scrawny boy up and down.

"I can barely survive myself," Anvin said, his voice heavy. "If I bring you, you shall surely die, too."

"I do not care," the boy replied immediately.

"Where I'm going," Anvin said, "lie the jaws of death. You would be squire to a dead man."

The boy grinned.

"I'd rather die fighting in the jaws of death than die here a slave."

Anvin finally smiled too, recognizing a proud defiance in the boy that reminded him of himself at that age. Finally, he nodded, and the boy, beaming, rushed forward and mounted the horse, settling behind Anvin.

Anvin kicked, and the two of them rode off, soon cutting through Pandesian lines, undetected, riding north, faster and faster, on their way, finally, to Andros.

Duncan, he thought, *wait for me.*

CHAPTER TWENTY ONE

As Kyra lay on the battlefield, withdrawing, preparing to die, a sound arose through the clamor, one that urged her to stay alive. It was a curious sound, a sound of men shrieking and falling on the field of battle, of chaos in the Pandesian ranks. It made no sense—and that, the mystery, forced her to hang on more than anything. Why, after all, would Pandesian soldiers be falling? It had been just her against their army. Who else could possibly be attacking them?

In her semi-conscious state, Kyra looked over to see something rippling through the ranks. It was a blur of motion, of light, moving so fast she could barely see it, and it caused enough disruption to make the soldier standing above her lower his sword and look away.

Kyra took advantage of his moment of distraction and leaned back and kicked him with all she had between the legs. The soldier keeled over, and moments later the whirling ball of light drove him to the ground. She saw a flash of metal, saw a blur of motion and a sword lowering, killing the soldier. Then she looked up, and she was utterly shocked at what she saw.

Kyle.

He sped through the ranks like lightning, raising his spear and felling soldiers in every direction, like a fish cutting through water. Pandesians fell all around him, none safe from his deadly blows, none fast enough to stop him, much less catch him. Kyra felt a flood of relief at the sight of him; more than that, she felt a rush of love. She was overflowing with gratitude. He had come back, she realized, for her.

Kyra desperately wanted to call out to him, to reach for him, but she was too weak, drifting in and out of consciousness. All she could do was watch as Kyle cut his way through the ranks, like a dream, taking out one row of soldiers after the next. She had never witnessed power like that. He was an unstoppable force, clearly of another race. He seemed invincible, like a wave of destruction, as hundreds of soldiers fell before him. Even the dark sorcerer's power seemed unable to stop him.

There came a lull in the fighting, and as Kyra opened her eyes, wondering how much time had passed, she looked out to see hundreds more bodies strewn on the battlefield. The entire first wave of Pandesians were dead. She could hardly believe it. There came the sound of a horn, though, and she looked up and saw something that made her blood run cold: thousands more Pandesians marched on the horizon, a force ten times the size of this, all coming to back up their men. She looked over and saw Kyle, bloody, breathing hard, clearly exhausted, and she knew that even he could not withstand another onslaught.

There followed the sound of another horn, rising up through the air. Yet, strangely enough, this was not the sound of the familiar horns of Escalon or Pandesia. She could not place it; she had never heard it before.

Kyra turned and looked back and her heart stopped as she saw the horizon behind her lined with thousands more soldiers—yet, even more disturbing, these were soldiers of another army. Another race. There, marching steadily toward over the hill, toward the capital, and toward the Pandesian army, were thousands of trolls. Those horns, Kyra realized with a start, were the trumpets of Marda. Of a nation of trolls. She could hardly believe it: their invasion had begun.

Two massive armies were about to face off with each other, and it so happened that Kyra and Kyle were stuck in the middle. There was no possible way, she realized, that Kyle could fight off both sides at once— and both sides, with eyes on him, clearly wanted him dead as the first act of war. Kyle saw it, too, his eyes wide with surprise, realizing at the same time that she did.

Kyle suddenly ran over to her and knelt by her side, gasping for breath. There was blood on his hands, his shoulders, his arms, and she, concerned, reached out to hug him. But even as she tried, her shoulders fell; her eyes were too heavy, and she was too weak from the loss of blood, her wounds.

A moment later, Kyra felt Kyle's smooth hands on her waist, then felt herself being lifted up into the air. It felt so good to be in his arms.

He set her down, stomach first, on Andor's back. She tried to open her eyes to see, yet, in and out of consciousness, she was too weak. She saw but a flash of images: Kyle's face, staring back, compassion in his eyes. Both armies closing in. And finally, Kyle gently holding her face in his hands.

"Go far from here," he said, his voice so soft. "Andor knows where. Never come back. And remember me."

Then he looked into her eyes until, finally, she was able to open them, just for a moment.

"I love you," he said.

Kyle leaned in and whispered into Andor's ear, and she tried to reach for him, to ask him not to leave. Yet she was too weak to utter the words.

Then Andor took off. He bolted with her on his back, Leo at his side. Kyra desperately tried to stop him. She did not want to run from this battlefield, nor did she want Kyle to remain back there for her sake, where he would surely die.

Yet she was too exhausted to stop Andor. There was nothing she could do but hold on as she found herself racing through the countryside, slumped over him, heading far away from here.

She mustered the strength to look back one last time, over her shoulder, the world bobbing up and down. She saw Kyle, now but a spec, surrounded, the armies closing in on him from both sides. He stood there proudly and raised his spear, unflinching, prepared to meet them both, prepared to wage a battle he knew he could not win. Kyra felt her heart torn inside as she knew he was remaining behind to distract them, to keep them away from her, to die for her sake.

CHAPTER TWENTY TWO

Vesuvius led the army of trolls as he charged for the Pandesians, raising his halberd high and letting out a great battle cry. He was eager for blood, and he could almost taste it. Before him lay a sight which set his heart on fire: a sea of blue and yellow, these Pandesians foolish enough to think they could stop Marda. He would kill each and every one of them.

As he approached, Vesuvius noticed that, oddly, they did not even seem to be charging for his trolls—instead, they all seemed fixated on attacking a single man. A boy, rather, with long golden hair, who moved through their ranks like a burst of light, attacking them from all sides, and who only stopped, briefly, to put a girl on a horse and send her away.

It was a confusing scene, and Vesuvius hardly knew what to make of it. Who was this boy who dared face off against an army of Pandesian forces? Who was the girl he had saved? Where had he sent her?

None of it mattered, though; Vesuvius would gladly kill anyone and anything in his way, and if they stood in the way of the capital, then the worse for them. The capital would be his. His ultimate goal, of course, was to raid the Tower of Kos and seize the Sword of Fire; but Andros was right on the way, and it was too valuable a prize to pass over. Besides, he was having too much fun destroying this countryside, one city at a time.

Although the sea of blue and yellow before him greatly outnumbered his trolls, Vesuvius had been desperate to do battle with them. Killing these humans in Escalon had been too easy; he craved a real foe. As he watched the odd battle ensue before him, though, he began to realize that that boy, the one who was beating them soundly but slowly losing strength, clearly must be important. Why else would they face off against him? And how else would he be able to fend them off?

He must, Vesuvius realized, be a very special prize for Pandesia— which meant he would also be a special prize for Marda. Vesuvius admired any warrior who could fight like that; this boy clearly had more backbone than his sorry army of trolls. He wanted him as a prize. He wanted him fighting for his nation.

"FORWARD!" Vesuvius shrieked.

Vesuvius charged forward, raising his halberd, salivating at the thought of battle, of bloodshed, hearing the thunderous footsteps of his nation behind him. As they closed in, the mysterious boy turned, and Vesuvius saw no fear in his glowing grey eyes, which surprised him. He had never before encountered an enemy who did not quake in fear at the sight of his grotesque face and body.

But he did see surprise. After all, the boy certainly could not have expected an army of trolls to bear down on him, to sandwich him between them and the Pandesian army. Vesuvius grinned wide, deciding to turn up the heat.

"ARROWS!" he shrieked.

Obediently, his front line of soldiers raised their bows and fired on command.

Vesuvius watched with delight as the sky blackened and the sea of arrows sailed for the boy. He anticipated the moment of the boy's death, of his being pierced by thousands of arrows, and he nearly squealed in delight. Perhaps now he would be afraid.

But as Vesuvius watched, he was shocked to see the boy stand there, unflinching, as if ready to embrace the arrows. And then, to Vesuvius's horror, the boy merely moved his arm at the last moment and swatted all the arrows away. They parted ways in the sky, falling all around him, many even sailing past him and killing Pandesian soldiers.

Vesuvius stared, dumbfounded. He had never seen anything like it in his life. Clearly, this was no human, but a boy of another race. Which would make an even more valuable prize.

The boy turned and stared at Vesuvius, as if singling him out, and the two locked eyes. Vesuvius took note of the fierceness in the boy's eyes, a fierceness that matched his own, and his curiosity deepened. He raised his halberd and doubled his speed, heading right for him. He loved a challenge, and finally, he had found a worthy opponent.

Vesuvius, just feet away, brought his halberd down for the boy's chest, aiming to split him in two. He could already feel the victory.

But to his surprise, the boy sidestepped, faster than he'd thought, raised his staff, and to Vesuvius's shock, swept it upwards and knocked Vesuvius back off his feet. It was a surprisingly powerful blow, stronger than any Vesuvius had ever received.

On his back, seeing stars, his head ringing, Vesuvius realized this was the first time he had been beaten in as long as he could remember. Now he really wanted to know: who was this boy? Now he was determined to capture this boy at all costs. He needed him—if he could control his own urge to kill him first.

Vesuvius's thousands of trolls closed in, surrounding the boy from all directions. The boy swung his staff, and Vesuvius saw sparks of light fly as the boy swatted away halberds as if they were toothpicks. He spun around and struck down his trolls ten at a time, making a mockery of them. Vesuvius was about to join the fray.

Yet before he could, he was forced to turn to the Pandesians, as there suddenly came a thunderous clash of armor and weaponry, the sea of blue and yellow meeting his trolls. Their attention distracted from the boy, both armies locked with each other. Humans shrieked and fell as his trolls, twice their size, raised their mighty halberds and chopped them in half, right through their armor.

And yet the Pandesians kept coming, relentless, like a stream of ants, with no regard to death. They were an army of slaves, with remorseless commanders, and it showed. Vesuvius admired their discipline, their complete disregard for life. Row after row of Pandesians surged forward, their ranks replenished as soon as one row was killed.

Enough of them eventually got through, keeping to their well-disciplined lines, and it was only a matter of time until the trolls, despite their greater size and strength, began to fall.

Vesuvius turned as a dozen Pandesian soldiers descended on him. He swung his halberd as their swords came down, chopping four swords in half in a single blow, then swung around in the same motion and chopped off four heads.

At the same time a dozen more soldiers jumped him from behind. As they tackled him to the ground, he spun and spread his massive arms, sending them flying back. He then elbowed them across the face, cracking jaws, hearing bones snap, a sound that gave him great joy.

Yet still a dozen more soldiers appeared, knocking him down, kicking him in the face, all over his body. He grabbed his halberd off the ground, swung around and chopped off their legs, killing half a dozen more.

An arrow then sailed down at him, barely missing.

Then another.

And another.

All around him, trolls began to fall. As Vesuvius looked to the horizon, he saw an endless sea rippling with yellow and blue. He knew he could kill thousands of them—but he finally realized it would not be enough. These Pandesians had *millions* of men. Their relentless troops were like an army of ants that would eventually crawl over and kill his nation. He knew he had to retreat. He had no choice. They could have Andros for now. The bigger prize, after all, was the Tower of Kos, the Sword, and lowering the Flames. Once he did that, it would allow millions of his men to enter. Then he could finish this war—on his own terms.

Vesuvius gestured to his commanders, and as he commanded them, for the first time in years, they sounded the horn of retreat. It was a noise that pained his ears.

Well disciplined, his soldiers turned and began to retreat. Yet as he turned to go, Vesuvius realized he could not leave without his prize. He returned his eyes to the boy, who was proudly attacking Pandesians and trolls on both sides, spinning in circles, fending them off. He could see the boy was exhausted, overextended, his powers drained, fighting too many soldiers in both directions. This boy was heroic and reckless.

Vesuvius knew he could not use a normal weapon on the boy—and he knew now that he did not want him dead. He was too valuable for that.

"THE BOY!" Vesuvius shouted to his elite soldiers.

A hundred of his best trolls turned and joined him as he raced for the boy. They surrounded him on all sides, all swinging halberds.

The boy fended off this surge of troops with his magical spear and staff, the clang of metal heavy in the air. As frustrated as he was, Vesuvius had to admit he also admired him. It had been a long time since he had encountered a warrior he actually admired.

Vesuvius realized quickly that even his elite men could not beat him— nor did they have much time, with the Pandesians closing in. He kept his men fighting, though, as a distraction. It gave him time to extract his Luathian net and creep up behind the boy. Crafted of strands of an ancient source, it was a weapon he reserved for very special situations—just like this.

Vesuvius pulled the net from the sack at his waist, rushed forward, and as he came up behind the boy, cast it in the air. It unfolded with an unearthly whistle, as if alive, and he watched in delight as it spread out and dropped down on the boy. It entangled him, magically contracting, shrinking around him, wrapping him up, constraining his arms. Within moments the boy, unable to move, fell to the ground.

He was his.

Vesuvius, thrilled, grabbed his prize by the waist and slung him over his shoulder.

"RETREAT!" he commanded.

He turned and ran, sprinting at full speed, as his nation of trolls followed. The Tower of Kos was somewhere south, the Devil's Finger lay before him, and with his newfound prize, his newest recruit, there would be no   stopping   him   now.

CHAPTER TWENTY THREE

His Most Glorious and Supreme Ra descended for the dungeons of Andros flanked by two dozen of his entourage, his boots echoing on the spiral stone staircase as he descended level after level. He reached the lowest levels and marched down dark stone corridors, lit only by distant shafts of sunlight, passing rows of iron bars. They were like most prisons he had been in: some prisoners rushed forward, shrieking, while others sat there silent, simmering with rage. Ra loved dungeons. They reminded him of his supreme power, of how everyone in the world was subservient to him.

Ra marched down the halls, ignoring them all, interested in only one person: the final prisoner in the final cell. Ra had made sure Duncan was kept in its deepest and darkest part. After all, he wanted to break this man more than anything.

Ra turned down corridor after corridor until he passed the last of the cells and reached one final cell at the very end. He stood before it and nodded, and several of his servants rushed forward and unlocked it for him.

The great iron gates squeaked open slowly.

"Leave me," Ra turned and commanded his men.

His entourage turned and marched from the corridors, taking up positions out of sight.

Ra entered the cell as the door slammed shut behind him. It was much darker in here, and as he walked through the darkness, filled with the sound of dripping water and scurrying rats, there, in a dark corner, he saw the man he had come to see. Duncan. There he sat, the leader of the great rebellion, the man rumored to be among the greatest warriors in all the world.

How pathetic. There he sat, shackled, on the ground like a dog. He sat unmoving, his eyes nearly shut from all the beatings he had received. Ra sighed. He had hoped for a more formidable opponent than this. Was there no one in the world left who was as strong as he?

And yet as Ra approached, Duncan looked up into the torchlight, right at him, and Ra recognized something in his eyes, some pride, some valor, some fearlessness, that impressed him. It was a look Ra saw rarely, and one that he relished when he did. Immediately he felt a kinship with this man, even if he was his enemy. Maybe he would not prove to be as disappointing as he thought.

Ra stopped a few feet before Duncan, towering over him. He savored the silence, the feeling of control over him.

"Do you know whom you face?" Ra asked, his voice authoritative and booming in the cell, echoing off the walls.

Ra waited for many seconds, yet Duncan did not respond.

"I am the Great and Holy Emperor of Pandesia, His Glorious Ra. I am the light of the sun, the beams of the moon, and the cradle of the stars. You are being afforded a great honor to be in my presence, an honor which few receive in a lifetime. When I enter a room people stand and bow down to me; whether chained or not, they lower their face to the ground. You will bow to me now, or you will meet your death."

A long silence followed. Finally, Duncan looked up and stared back, defiant.

Ra stood there, waiting impatiently. He craved deference from the last surviving man who had dared show him defiance. Having Duncan bow down to him would be like having Escalon bow to him, would show Ra that there was not a soul left in this land who dared defy him.

Yet, to his fury, Duncan did not bow.

Finally, Duncan cleared his throat.

"I bow to no one," Duncan said, his voice weak. "No man and no god. And you certainly are no god. Wait for me to bow to you, and you shall be waiting a very long time."

Ra reddened. He had never faced such impunity.

"Are you prepared to meet your death?" Ra asked.

Duncan stared back, unflappable.

"I have faced death many times," he replied. "It is a familiar friend. All whom I love are dead. It would come to me now as a welcome relief."

Ra saw the spark in this man's eyes, and he sensed his words were true. He heard the authority in his voice, the authority of a man who had commanded men, and it made him respect him even more.

Ra cleared his throat and sighed.

"I came down here," he replied, "to see the face of my enemy. To let you know firsthand what I have done to your once-great country. It is all in my hands now. All subjugated. Every last village and city. Your daughter, Kyra, is being hunted down now and will be ours soon. I will take great joy and pride in having her as my personal slave."

Ra smiled wide as he could see the anger flash in Duncan's face. Finally, he was getting to him.

"Your great warriors are all killed or captured," Ra continued, wanting to pain him, "and nothing remains of the Escalon that once was. Soon it will not even be a memory, for I shall rename it. It will be but another outpost of Pandesia. Your name, your exploits, your warriors, the life you've lived—all of it will be wiped from the history books. *You* will be nothing, not even a shell, not even a memory. And those who remember you will all be dead, too."

Ra grinned, unable to contain his joy.

"I came down here because I wanted to see your face when I told you," he concluded.

There came a long silence, Ra waiting, trembling with anticipation, seeing the range of emotions swirl through Duncan's face.

Finally, Duncan replied.

"I don't need memories," he said, his voice raspy yet still defiant. "I don't need history books. I know the life I lived. I know *how* I have lived. And so do the people who have lived it with me. Whether I am dead or forgotten makes no difference to me. You say you have taken everything away. Yet you forget one thing: our spirit remains intact. And that can never been taken. That is the one thing you shall never possess. And the anger that that gives you, that is what shall give me joy at my death."

Ra felt an intense wave of rage. He took a deep breath and scowled down at this defiant creature.

"In the morning," Ra said, trembling with anger, "when they come to take you to your death, you will stand in the public square and proclaim to all of Andros that you were wrong. That I am the supreme ruler. That you defer to me. If you do so, I will not torture you, and you will die a quick and painless death. If you are convincing, I may even let you live and return to you the rulership of your land."

This was the moment when Ra expected Duncan, like all his other prisoners in all his other lands, to finally give in.

But to Ra's surprise, Duncan continued to stare back defiantly.

"Never," Duncan replied.

Ra glared back. In a rage, he drew his sword and raised it, his hands shaking. More than anything he craved to chop off his head right now. Yet he forced himself to refrain, wanting to see him tortured publicly instead.

Ra threw down his sword, and it landed with a clang. He turned and burst out of the cell, eager for dawn, for Duncan's death, and for Escalon to be his.

CHAPTER TWENTY FOUR

Kavos paced the holding pen amidst the crowd of soldiers, Bramthos, Seavig and Arthfael beside him, all of them prisoners of war, all desperate to get out. Beside him were hundreds of men, his men, Duncan's men, Seavig's men, all proud and noble soldiers, all who had followed Duncan into war and been forced to surrender. He could hardly conceive that it had come to this, that they were all at the mercy of Pandesia.

Kavos fumed. It had been a mistake to surrender to these Pandesians. Better to have gone down to their deaths fighting. Duncan had been led away, it pained him as he wondered what had become of him. Was he alive? Dead? Being tortured?

Kavos had never surrendered before, not once in his life, under any circumstances, and he did so this time only grudgingly. He had done so only at Duncan's command, had only laid down his arms because thousands of other soldiers had done so as well. They had all been corralled into this pen outside the capital, awaiting their fate, day after day, with no end in sight. Were they going to be released? Would there be an amnesty? Would they be enslaved in the Pandesian army? Or was Pandesia waiting to put them all to death?

Kavos paced, as he had every day, waiting to hear their fate. He looked over at the thousands of dejected soldiers in here, standing or sitting or pacing, being held in this huge stone courtyard, iron bars caging them in on all sides. They were hardly a mile outside the capital, and he looked out and saw the Pandesian flag flying boldly over the city gates. He burned. He wanted just one more chance to boldly attack the Pandesians. He did not care if he died in the process—he just did not want to die like this.

More than anything, Kavos wanted to find and free Duncan. Duncan was a good man and a good warlord, who had just made one mistake in being too trusting, in taking men for their word. Not all men were like he.

"You think they're still alive?" came a voice.

Kavos turned to see Seavig standing beside him, looking at him, concern across his face. Kavos sighed.

"Duncan was not born to die," he said.

"Death holds no grip on him," Bramthos added, coming up beside him. "He has escaped it too many times. If he dies, then what is best in all of us dies with him."

"Yet his sons were killed," Seavig chimed in. "That could strip away his will to live."

"True," Arthfael said, joining them. "Yet he has another son to live for. And a daughter."

97

"Shall we just stand here and wait then?" asked Bramthos. "Wait for the Pandesians to decide our fates? To come and kill us all?"

They all exchanged uncomfortable glances.

"They won't kill us," Seavig said. "If they were to kill us, wouldn't they have already?"

Kavos shrugged as they all looked to him.

"Perhaps not," Kavos replied. "After all, there lies a value in killing us publicly."

"Or enslaving us," Arthfael added, "breaking us up into their armies and sending us overseas."

As they all stood there, concerned, a sudden cheer cut through the air. Kavos and the others turned and looked out through the iron bars and he saw, in the distance, a large group of Pandesian soldiers cheering, waving the banner of Pandesia. He watched the jubilant soldiers, wondering what was happening.

He called out to the guard standing just beyond the wall.

"What's happened?"

The soldier turned and grinned at him.

"Congratulations," the soldier said. "Your King is dead."

Kavos felt a pit in his stomach as he wracked his brain, trying to understand. Did he mean Duncan?

Then, suddenly, he realized: Enis. The usurper.

"None of us are safe," Seavig said. "If they have killed him already, surely they won't spare us."

They all looked to each other with grim faces, and Kavos knew he was right. They did not respect the rule of law. Death was coming for them all.

"Night falls," said another, looking out past the setting sun, to the torches being lit. "Perhaps they will kill us, too, tomorrow."

"Let's not give them the chance then," Kavos said, forming an idea.

They all looked at him.

"We have no weapons," Seavig said. "What can we do?"

"We have our hands," Kavos replied. "And we have our minds. Sometimes that is all one needs."

They looked back with puzzled expressions, and Kavos, an idea forming, walked to the cell bars.

"You there!" he called out to the guard again. "We need help!"

The Pandesian guard, pacing in the distance, looked his way suspiciously.

"What help could you possibly need?" he asked.

"I have something here," he improvised, "something that the Supreme Ra will be eager to see."

The guard furrowed his brow and then turned and approached, stopping a few feet away.

98

"If you're wasting my time," he said gruffly, "I will kill you. And your friends." He scowled. "So what is it?"

Kavos swallowed, thinking fast. He needed the guard to get closer.

"You can bring it to him yourself and be the hero," Kavos said. "All I want in return is more provisions."

"You'll be lucky if I don't give you death," the guard snapped. "Now show it to me."

Kavos, suddenly remembering the jewel in his satchel, the one his wife had given him before he'd left for war, took out a cloth from his sack, unfolded it, and revealed a sparkling red ruby.

The guard, intrigued, stepped forward, as Kavos hoped he would, and stopped before the iron bars.

"Hand it through," he demanded.

"Surely," Kavos answered.

Kavos reached out with the jewel, putting it through the bars, and as the guard reached, Kavos dropped it. The guard squatted down to pick it up, and as he did, Kavos kicked him as hard as he could, through the bars, in the face, knocking him out.

There came a sudden commotion as all the prisoners around him rushed forward, excited. Kavos lunged through the bars and grabbed the body, just able to reach it. He then dragged him forward, reached for the guard's belt and grabbed his keys. All the men around him cheered as he quickly unlocked it with shaking hands.

The heavy iron squeaked as they pushed it open.

Kavos stopped at the cell door, looking out, seeing the Pandesians in the distance who luckily hadn't spotted them yet. All the prisoners stopped at the door behind him, unsure. Kavos turned and faced them.

"Men," he called out, "we're unarmed. We have two choices. We can flee to our homes, escape from the capital, and go as far and as fast as we can. Or we can do what warriors do, what men of Escalon do: kill these invaders, strip their arms, and rescue our commander! We will likely die trying. But we shall die with honor! Are you with me?!"

There came a great cheer. As one, the prisoners stampeded out of the gate, a unified force, all rushing for the Pandesians, all prepared to fight to the death. They would either die on this field, or Andros would be theirs.

Duncan, Kavos thought. *Hang in there. We're coming for you.*

CHAPTER TWENTY FIVE

Aidan stood with Motley atop the makeshift stage, a huge wooden platform in the center of Andros, and he looked out at the sea of faces. He stood there, frozen. For the first time in his life, he experienced stage fright. He had never gone anywhere near a stage before, had never even met an actor before meeting Motley, and as he stood there, part of the play, looking out at the crowd, everyone looking back at him, he had never felt so self-conscious in his life. He wanted to curl up and die.

As he stood there, unable to remember his line, Aidan had a whole new respect for actors. In their own way, he realized, they were fearless warriors. It took courage to face this crowd of strangers, more courage than he had, more courage, even, than it took his father and his men to raise their swords.

Motley turned and faced him, clearly annoyed, and repeated his line:

"Do you really think Escalon can serve him?" he prodded.

Aidan had tunnel vision. The world slowed as he saw several actors in one corner of the stage juggling multicolored balls, and several actors in another corner twirling flaming torches across the stage. He knew he had a part in this play, but he just could not, for the life of him, remember what it was.

Finally, Motley must have realized he was blanking, because he stepped up and draped a hand on Aidan's shoulder.

"I can see that you do," Motley boomed out to the crowd, saving him. "I am glad to serve the Supreme and Holy Ra, as are we all. He has glorified our homeland with his visit. Don't you think?"

Aidan knew this was his cue, that he was supposed to say something. But he forgot what it was. He felt all the eyes on him, and he wished he were invisible. This was a stupid plan, he realized now, thinking they could use their entertainment to distract the Pandesians, to get them into the heart of the capital, closer to his father, to save him. It had gotten them closer, but Aidan didn't see how this could ever work. It had allowed them access to the center of the capital, and Motley had been right: it seemed the entire city was riveted. It was the distraction he needed. Yet he couldn't remember, with all these eyes upon him, what he was supposed to do.

"Yes," he finally said, his voice cracking.

The crowd burst into laughter, clearly realizing that Aidan had forgot his lines, and Aidan reddened; he had never felt more humiliated.

"And you will serve him forever?" Motley prodded, secretly nodding yes.

"Yes," Aidan said again.

Motley faced the crowd and grinned.

"A man of many words!" he called out.

The crowd roared with laughter.

A group of actors suddenly rushed forward and joined them on stage, juggling torches, signaling that this part of the play was over. As they did, Motley gestured to Aidan, who rushed over to him.

"Now's the time," Motley whispered urgently. "Move quickly!"

Aidan snapped back to the present, remembered their master plan, why they were here in the first place. With the crowd distracted, he quickly slinked away, taking cover behind the new actors, and exited from the rear of the stage.

Aidan's heart was slamming as he bolted from the stage, jumping down, hitting the ground hard and stumbling to the ground. He scrambled to his knees and ran to a dark corner behind the stage, where he collected himself, breathing hard, sweating.

He looked everywhere, his palms sweaty, trying to recall the plan. It was hard to think straight.

His father. The dungeons. The guards....

White, waiting in the shadows of the stage, immediately came up beside him. Aidan knelt down before him and stroked his head.

"You stay here, boy," he said. "I can't have you coming where I'm going. Wait for Motley. He'll bring you."

White licked his face in return.

Aidan realized he had no time left to lose. He burst back into action, heart pounding with excitement, realizing how close his father was. He sprinted down dark alleys, twisting and turning through the back streets of Andros, heading toward the low, stone building in the distance which he knew held the dungeon.

He finally stopped nearby and crouched in the shadows, breathing hard, as he looked over and studied a Pandesian soldier standing guard at the imposing iron gates to the dungeon. Aidan racked his brain, wondering how to get past the guard. He had hoped, with the whole city watching the play, that the guards would be, too. But he was wrong. He could not overpower this man, and he didn't see any way past him.

Aidan thought hard and realized he needed to cause a distraction. He reached down and felt the pouch of silver coins at his waist, the ones Motley had given him, just in case. He crept closer along the wall and when he was but a few feet away, he reached out and flung the sack with all his might.

It landed in the courtyard, about ten feet from the guard, and the silver coins spilled out and clinked all over the cobblestone.

The soldier jumped. He rushed over to the noise, and Aidan held his breath while he looked about suspiciously.

This was his chance. Aidan raced for the open gate, his heart slamming. He began to rush through it—when suddenly he heard footsteps right behind him and felt a rough hand on his shoulder. He felt himself being yanked back, and he turned to see the angry face of the Pandesian soldier, dressed in blue and yellow armor, staring him down.

"Where do you think you're going?" he demanded. "Who are you?"

Aidan stood there, speechless, unsure what to say.

The soldier leaned in close, pulled a dagger from his waist, and began to raise it. Aidan cringed, realizing this would end badly. He had no way out, and didn't know what to say.

"You were trying to sneak into the dungeons. Why?" the soldier demanded. "Trying to rescue someone, are you? Who?"

Aidan struggled to break free, but it was no use. The soldier was too strong. He raised his dagger, preparing to slice Aidan's throat, and Aidan was certain his time had come. What pained him most was not the thought of dying, but rather being so close to freeing his father—and failing.

Aidan spotted motion out of the corner of his eye, and then it all happened so fast; he saw long, strawberry hair, then saw a short girl grab the soldier's arm and snap his wrist. The soldier shrieked, dropping his knife.

The girl immediately grabbed it and in one quick motion, sank it into his heart.

The soldier gasped and dropped to his knees, a shocked expression on his face, seeming more surprised that a young, small girl could kill him than by the fact that he was dying. The girl pulled out the dagger and quickly sliced his throat, and he dropped down to the ground face first, dead.

Aidan stood there, stunned, realizing his life had been saved and not understanding why, or who this person was. She faced him, and as he looked closely, he began to recognize the girl's features. Beneath the dirt on her face and clothes she was disarmingly pretty, about his age, with sparkling blue eyes and strong cheekbones. He knew her, but could not remember from where.

"Don't you remember me?" she asked.

Aidan shook his head, trying.

"You helped me once," she said. "You gave me your coins."

She held out a sack of gold coins, and he suddenly remembered. The beggar girl. The one he had given all his money to. *Cassandra.*

She smiled.

"I meant what I said," Cassandra said, "about paying you back. Consider us even."

Aidan looked at her with overwhelming gratitude, unsure what to say. He glanced back over his shoulder, saw the open cell to the dungeons, and he knew this was his chance.

"Don't most people try to run *away* from a dungeon?" she asked with a smirk.

"My father's in there," Aidan replied, in a rush.

"And you really think you will free him?" she asked. "That he will be unguarded?"

Aidan realized as she uttered the words how stupid his plan was. But it was too late now. There was no other choice.

He shrugged.

"I must try," he said, preparing to go. "It's my father."

She examined him, as if wondering if he were crazy, then finally shook her head.

"Okay then," she said. "Let's do it."

Aidan's eyes lifted in surprise.

"Why would you help me?" he asked.

She smiled back.

"I like the risk," she said, "and I like the cause. And I *really* hate the Pandesians."

There came a commotion and Aidan turned and saw over his shoulder a dozen Pandesian soldiers appearing from the courtyard, rushing right for them. He looked toward the dungeons, and was horrified to see a dozen more soldiers charging from the other side.

He turned and looked at Cassandra, and she looked back at him with an equal expression of horror.

They were trapped.

CHAPTER TWENTY SIX

Kyra walked slowly through the mist, arms out at her side, as she entered an obscured forest path. She passed low, thick trees with gnarled branches, twisting and turning, reaching out for her. They created an archway, a path covering her head, leading deeper and deeper into the gloom and fog. It was a path she felt she had been walking forever.

The path opened and Kyra found herself in a small clearing, the fog thicker here. Before her sat a small stone cottage, torchlight flickering from inside, a beacon amidst the thickening fog. Kyra wondered who could be inside, who could live in such an eerie place, here in the midst of nowhere, inside a mysterious, ancient forest.

Slowly, its weathered, oak door creaked open, and there emerged a figure who stood before her, staring back, but a few feet away. Kyra blinked and could hardly believe her eyes. It was *her*. She faced *herself*.

Standing there was an exact replica of herself, facing her, blinking back. It was the most frightening thing Kyra had ever seen.

"Are you worthy?" her replica asked.

Kyra stared back, wondering. It was her face she stared at; it was her voice, her gestures, her body, and she did not know how to respond.

"Are you worthy?" the girl repeated.

"I don't understand," Kyra replied.

"Are you worthy of becoming the warrior Escalon needs you to be?" the girl asked.

Kyra blinked, confused.

"I *am* worthy," Kyra finally replied.

The girl suddenly pulled out a staff, and Kyra was shocked to see it was just like hers. Kyra reached for her own staff, as the girl suddenly charged and attacked her.

Kyra blocked it, the clanging of metal echoing through the forest, as the girl swung for her again and again. The two fought, perfectly matched, driving each other back and forth through the clearing, neither able to gain an advantage. They anticipated every blow, and neither could find an opening.

Kyra, drenched in sweat, felt locked in a battle that seemed as if it would last forever. She was battling herself, she realized, and she did not know how to do that.

Just as she thought the fighting would never end Kyra lowered her staff just a bit, and suddenly, to her surprise, her staff was knocked from her hand. Her replica unscrewed the end of her staff, revealing a blade, and suddenly stepped forward and stabbed Kyra in the gut.

Kyra gasped, the pain so severe she couldn't even speak.

"Are you worthy?" the girl asked, staring intensely into her eyes.

Kyra gasped as she stared back, speechless, knowing she was dying.

Kyra sat up, shrieking, covered in a cold sweat, reaching for her stomach. She breathed hard, looking all about her, and it took her several minutes to realize she had been dreaming.

Kyra ran a hand over her stomach, and she still felt the pain from her dream, as it if were real. She massaged it, trying to find the wound, and was baffled to find none.

Kyra felt she was lying on something uncomfortable, and she looked down and saw hard stone beneath her. Her body aching, she sat up, twisted and turned, and looked all around, disoriented, wondering where she was. It was twilight, and as she peered into the light, the landscape so foreign, it took her a few moments to realize she was in a place she had never been before. She blinked several times, trying to remember.

She recalled a battle. Fighting against the Pandesians. Trying to reach Andros, to save her father. She had been surrounded, outnumbered, and she had been growing weak. She recalled being knocked down, losing consciousness, and then…Kyle appearing. Helping her.

Kyra vaguely remembered being put on the back of Andor, and as she heard a snort, she wheeled. Her heart leapt with delight to see Andor, chewing a patch of moss about ten feet away; at the same time, she felt something soft and furry lean against her, and she looked to her other side to find Leo licking her palm. She was relieved to her old friends here, with her.

Kyle had rescued her, she realized. He had put her on Andor and had sent her away, far from the battlefield. But to where?

Kyra felt a rush of guilt at the thought of abandoning Kyle back there, leaving him alone to fight off both armies. There was no way he could survive—and he must have known that. He had remained behind as a distraction, so that she could flee safely. He had sacrificed himself so that she could live. The thought of it killed her. She would give anything to be back there now, by his side.

Kyra looked around and as the fog cleared, saw she was standing in the midst of endless stone, caving statues, crumbling walls. It was a sprawling ruin, she realized, an ancient city that no longer was. Only foundations were left intact. It was an eerie, abandoned place, a haunted place. It had all been perfectly preserved, untouched for thousands of years, and in some ways it felt like walking through a graveyard.

She stood there, wondering where she was. It was the most exotic place she had ever been, a place that had clearly not seen visitors for thousands of years, the blueprint of a city that was once magnificent. And, standing in the midst of it, she had never felt more alone.

Kyra took her first step, seeing only ruins in every direction, realizing she was far from anything and would have to navigate her way through this city. She walked slowly in the rubble, rocks crunching beneath her feet, Leo beside her and Andor following. She looked out and was amazed at how vast this place was. This city was mystical, breathtaking, stretching for miles in every direction. She could hear the faint crashing of waves in the distance, and on the horizon, could see the vast Sea of Sorrow, its waves crashing at the cliffs far below. This city, up high, on a plateau, was perched at the edge of the ocean.

Kyra took it all in as she walked, rubbing her hand along the smooth ancient stone, so grateful to be alive. Her body hurt with each step, filled with aches and pains from the battle, yet she had not died, and she had Kyle to thank for that.

As she passed through a crumbling stone arch, an ancient gateway, she turned and looked up, and in the distance, towering over everything, she saw the one tall structure that remained in the city. It appeared to be a large, stone temple, some of its walls collapsing, and it was framed on either side by hundred foot stone statues, of women wearing laurel headdresses and with arms stretched out and palms up to the sky. It seemed like a holy place.

Kyra suddenly realized: the Lost Temple. The place of her mother's birth. The once-capital of Escalon. She had made it.

Kyra felt something special about this place, a mystical energy that hung in the air. It was like a vapor that clung to everything, the dirt, the stones. She could feel that this was a place of power, could feel that it had once been the greatest capital of the world. Yet she sensed something more. This was a sacred place. A place not inhabited by humans, but by those of another race. She could feel it in the very fabric of the air, in the touch of the stones, the electrifying feeling she got with each step she took.

Kyra had always heard of the Lost Temple growing up, a sacred place, the one place in Escalon where mortals feared to go. It was said that spirits walked the grounds here, lingered in the air, and that those few who were brave enough to venture here never returned.

Gales of wind whipped through, whistling off the ocean, off the rocks, and Kyra turned frequently, every time thinking she heard someone behind her, someone whispering at her. Yet there was no one.

She felt a chill. This was, indeed, a city of ghosts.

Kyra walked and walked, crisscrossing the city, making her way toward the temple, lured by the sound of the waves crashing in the distance. She did not know exactly what she was searching for, yet she knew, somehow, that she was exactly where she was meant to be.

As she hiked, Kyra could not help but feel that she was searching for her mother. She felt her mother's spirit hanging in the air here, guarding her, guiding her steps. Had her mother truly lived here? The thought thrilled her. Could she be here now?

As Kyra walked, she felt as if she were tracing the steps of her mother's life, and she wondered what life had been like for her mother here. Images flashed through her mind. She saw her most recent battle, killing Pandesians; she saw Theos, the powerful beast she had loved, flying somewhere high above; she saw her training with Alva; and she saw, most of all, persistent images of her mother, just out of reach. Her mother was here in this place, Kyra could feel it, and she felt closer to her than ever.

As she walked, winding her way through partial walls of collapsed stone, running her hand along them, Kyra spotted shards of ancient pottery on the ground—and she stopped as she saw an unusual object hidden in the debris. She picked it up, wiped years of dust off it, and she was stunned to realize she was holding an ancient sword. She raised it high, and it crumbled to pieces in her hand, collapsing into a cloud of dust. It must have sat there, she realized, for thousands of years.

Kyra walked and walked, drawn inexorably to the temple, keeping it in her line of vision and making her way toward it. As she approached, she looked up at the hundreds of worn stone steps at its base, the temple perched atop them on a wide stone plateau, looking as if it reached the sky. Kyra began to ascend, putting one foot before the other, the stone so smooth, clearly worn from thousands of years of use, and of ocean spray.

The more she ascended, the more Kyra was afforded a towering view of the city, the cliffs, and the ocean beyond. Finally reaching the top, she turned and saw the entire city spread out beneath her. It was breathtaking. Kyra felt as if she were on top of the world. Even amidst its decay, she could see the lines of the city that once was, its beautiful symmetry, and she could only imagine how grand a capital it was. Beyond it the beautiful waters of the Sorrow sparkled in the sunset, as if alive, framing it all.

Kyra turned and looked up and examined the temple, a massive stone structure rising still higher into the sky. Before her was a huge arch, carved into the stone, an entry into the temple. If there was ever a door, it disappeared centuries ago. Strangely enough, she could see two torches burning inside. She wondered how they could be lit, and she realized it was magic. She wondered at just how mystical this place was. She felt as if she were in another realm, wrangling with forces she did not understand.

Kyra turned, standing on the broad stone plateau, and looked out over the city. The ocean winds caressed her as she stared out into the sunset.

"Mother!" she called out, her voice echoing, carried by the wind. "Where are you?"

There came nothing but the howling of the wind and the crashing of the waves.

"Who am I?" she cried out.

Again, no response.

"Mother! I've come all this way to find you. Show yourself to me! Tell me who I am. Teach me!"

And yet still, to Kyra's dismay, there came nothing but silence.

Kyra, exhausted, weary from the battles, still covered with bruises, sank to her knees on the stone. She sat back on her feet, resting her hands in her lap, and closed her eyes. Feeling the cool ocean winds caress her face, she sat there as the sun sank.

She closed her eyes and tried to go inside herself. She did not understand this place; yet she sensed it was the key. It was the key to finding her mother. To unlocking her power. To understanding herself, her destiny. To saving Escalon.

Yet she did not know how to unravel it.

Kyra did not know how many hours passed as she knelt there. She sensed day turn to night, and against the monotony of crashing waves and howling wind, she rocked slowly and began to lose all track of time. She felt herself entering a deep meditation, going deeper within than she ever had before.

When she finally, slowly, opened her eyes, the sky was black. She looked up, and in the blackness she saw a sky filled with twinkling stars, and a rising full moon, the color of blood. Behind her, the two flickering torches never died.

Kyra knelt there, feeling hopelessly lost. Unsure of everything she knew. She reached the depths of uncertainty.

And in that moment of true uncertainty, a voice began to come to her. She began to see something in the darkness, slowly emerging, ascending the stairs, approaching her.

It was a person.

She saw her face, and, with a shock, she knew.

It was her mother.

CHAPTER TWENTY SEVEN

Kavos led the charge as hundreds of Duncan's men rallied behind him, all liberated after their escape from prison. They had the carefree shouts and cries of men who knew they had nothing to lose, who knew they could lose their lives at any moment—and likely would—as they charged recklessly into the heart of the capital, to a near certain death against thousands of better-armed Pandesians.

But that was what valor was all about, Kavos felt. Beside him charged Bramthos, Seavig and Arthfael, and he could see on their faces that they would not flinch from the enemy, either, would not even hesitate to throw themselves into battle. Indeed, since they had broken loose, they had already had several skirmishes with Pandesian battalions, fighting dozens of men here and there. A few of their own men had fallen, but mostly they had swept through the city like a wave of destruction, catching the Pandesians off guard, none of them slowing, using their momentum to kill and run and kill again.

Kavos raised his pilfered halberd as they turned a corner and surprised several dozen Pandesian soldiers, all with their backs to him. He hacked two of them down, as did Bramthos, Seavig and Arthfael beside him, before the others began to take notice and face them. Kavos, leading the fray, found himself defending as several Pandesians swung at him. He raised his halberd and turned it sideways, blocking blows from two sides. He leaned back and kicked one soldier in the chest, then spun around and chopped off another Pandesian's head. He was fighting for his life, and there was no time to lose.

The battle was vicious, hand to hand, the fighting thick. At first, the Pandesians rushed forward boldly, filled with their typical arrogance, clearly thinking the battle was theirs, that they would quickly dispatch these rogue prisoners crazy enough to make one last desperate charge into the city. However, Kavos and his men were determined, their backs to the wall. They rushed forward, in row after row, all giving it their all, hurling spears, slashing swords, smashing soldiers with shields. They came in like a wave, fast and furious, and they disregarded the body space between the lines. They came in so fast and so close, they actually wrestled some Pandesians down to the ground, preventing the Pandesians from having the time and space they needed to regroup.

The strategy worked. Soon, the Pandesians were in disarray. Half of their ranks were dead, compared to only a handful of Kavos' men, and the men that remained began to panic. They fought half-heartedly, until finally they turned, stumbling over each other, and fled.

Kavos and his men chased them down, not giving them a second chance to regroup, hurling spears into their backs and hacking them down. They fought like men possessed, men fighting for their lives.

Soon all was still, as the group of Pandesians lay dead, their bodies strewn throughout the capital. Kavos' men wasted no time in scouring the battlefield and salvaging their weapons, dropping their crude swords and shields for even nicer ones. Step by step, body by body, Duncan's men were becoming a professional army again.

Reinvigorated, Duncan's men let out a shout of victory and continued running throughout the capital, turning down street after street in the thick night, determined that nothing should stop them until they reached Duncan's dungeon and freed their commander.

CHAPTER TWENTY EIGHT

Merk pulled his shirt tight around his neck as he hiked, lowering his head, trying to shield himself from the incessant gales of wind that tore at his skin. The wind howled off the Sea of Tears on one side of him and the Bay of Death on the other, swaying him back and forth like a rag doll as he trekked endlessly, as he had been for days, between the two bodies of water, down the narrow, barren peninsula known as the Devil's Finger.

It was a name that inspired fear in most of Escalon, the one place that most Escalonites feared to go. They had little reason to. It was a barren, rock-strewn appendage to the bountiful land, a place one went to slip to one's death. Merk slipped and slid on its moss-covered boulders, all slick with ocean spray, making his way slowly and treacherously down the most notorious stretch of land in all of Escalon. Barely able to steady himself, he looked up at this bizarre peninsula of boulders stretching to the horizon, and wondered if this hell would ever end. He doubted he would survive it. This peninsula, if possible, was even worse than its reputation.

A place of legend—and of fear—the Devil's Finger was one of the few places in Escalon that Merk had never yearned to go. It jutted out of the mainland and reached to the far southeastern corner of Escalon like an appendage that never should have existed. "Peninsula" was too hospitable a name for it. It was nothing more than a barren stretch of rock, mostly slick and jagged, sandwiched between two bodies of tumultuous water.

Merk cursed as he slipped again, scraping a knee for the hundredth time. He had already twisted both ankles and wrists as he fell time and again, picking his way through each rock. He had created a sort of system, turning his ankles and raising his arms to give himself balance, leaning forward to catch himself on his hands when he slipped. This was an awful, nasty place, a place that no humans should ever live. It was too aptly named.

Merk knew, though, that he had no choice but to venture on. After crossing all of Escalon, this was the final leg to his trip, the last stretch between him and the Tower of Kos. Just reaching this peninsula had taken nearly all he had, his having to cross southeastern Escalon alone after he parted ways with Kyle, then skirt the peaks of Kos and hike alongside the Thusius. All of that trekking, just to arrive here, on this peninsula. This was probably why, he reasoned, most pilgrimaged to the Tower of Ur, not Kos. Kos was always rumored to be too barren, too desolate, too forgotten, to hold the Sword. Everyone had always assumed that it was the tower of distraction.

Yet as he searched the horizon, Merk knew otherwise. All the legends had been wrong. The legendary Sword of Fire lay where no one suspected it to be. Merk knew it was only a matter of time until the trolls found out, and he knew that he was racing the clock, with each step he took, to beat them there, to secure the sword before they could reach it.

Merk scanned the horizon again, hoping for some sign—any sign—of the peninsula's end. He hoped to see the outline of the tower, even if faint.

Yet there was nothing. Just more rock, with no end in sight. He was exhausted, worn to the bone, and yet it seemed he had still days more to go.

Merk looked out to his left and saw the Sea of Tears, its currents vicious, its huge waves smashing into the rocky shores of the Devil's Finger, sending up rolling waves of mist and foam. He felt the spray around his ankles, washing the stone beneath him, making him lose his balance. He did not know what was louder, the crashing of the waves or the gales of wind which kept him off balance.

Merk looked the other way, to his right, yet that sight offered no reprieve; there were the black, murky waters of the legendary Bay of Death. It, too, had vicious currents, yet these currents swirled, making a frothing collection of whirlpools. The bay was dotted with these whitecaps all the way to the horizon, the bright white a stark contrast to its black waters, stirred up by the constant gales of wind. For Merk, seeing those black waters was even more disconcerting than the waves smashing into the peninsula from the Sorrow. It was as if the two bodies of water were trying to destroy this narrow piece of land with all their might.

Merk turned to the path before him, looking ahead as he thought he heard an odd noise. Yet he saw nothing.

The sound came again, though, a distant sound, almost like a horn, and this time he looked back over his shoulder—and his heart fell as he spotted something on the horizon. There was the faintest outline of an army of banners, and as the distant horn sounded again, Merk knew, with dread, what it was: Marda. The trolls had already reached the Devil's Finger. They were making better time than he thought.

Merk turned back ahead and doubled his pace. He had a day's start on them, but they were gaining and could overtake him. It would be a race to the finish, to see who could reach the Tower of Kos and secure the Sword first.

Merk hurried forward, ignoring the hunger pangs in his stomach, the blisters on his toes, the exhaustion that nearly shut his eyes. He had to reach the Tower of Kos no matter what it took, to save Escalon, to redeem himself from his past. Despite it all, it felt good to finally have a cause, to have a true purpose in life.

Merk hiked and hiked, hour following hour, the sun growing high in the sky, blinding him from its haze through the ocean mist. He ascended the top of the highest boulder he had seen, eager for the new vantage point, filled with hope that, once at its top, he might finally spot the tower.

But he was crestfallen as he looked out and saw nothing but more boulders, more false peaks. It looked from here as if nothing but barren rock covered the world.

Merk stood there, out of breath, and leaned on his staff to rest for a moment—when suddenly he heard a new noise that made his hair stand on end. It was a clattering, and sounded like a crab skittering across rock.

He turned, on edge, and searched the boulders beneath him, wondering if he were hearing things. After all, there had been no signs of life on the entire journey, and it had not occurred to him that anything could even survive out here in these barren conditions. After all, what could they possibly feed on?

But then it came again, an unsettling clattering noise, and as Merk searched the rocks again, a gust of wind carried away the mist, and this time he saw something that made his blood run cold. In a crack between boulders, there slowly emerged an enormous claw. It was a crab's claw, yet bigger than any claw he had ever laid eyes upon. It stretched and stretched, at least ten feet long.

There emerged another claw, then another, and Merk watched in horror as there emerged from the fissure a monstrous crab, thirty feet wide, overshadowing him. Merk froze as he stood there and looked up at it. With its black shell and red, beady eyes, it lifted its head and scowled down at him, opening its jaws and hissing, displaying rows of jagged teeth.

It then skittered across the boulders, right for him.

The creature moved surprisingly fast, and Merk stood there, frozen in fear, not expecting this, and having no idea what to do. He had no room to maneuver, even if he wanted to. It lunged right for him, claws out. A moment later Merk felt an awful pain on his shin, and he looked down to see one of its claws grabbing him, pinching him.

The crab hoisted him into the air, and as Merk dangled by one leg, it opened its mouth wide and pulled him close, preparing to swallow him whole. Merk saw the rows of teeth looming, and he knew he was about to die in the most awful way imaginable.

By some grace of god, Merk's instincts kicked in at the last moment, and he reached out with his staff, turned it, and jammed it vertically inside the creature's mouth. The crab tried to close its mouth and was furious to find it jammed.

Merk, still dangling, reached into his belt, drew his sword, spun around, and with one huge effort, plunged it with both hands into one of the crab's eyes.

The crab shrieked as green pus shot out of it, and it released its grip on Merk. Merk landed hard on the rocks, winded, feeling as if his bones were breaking. He rolled and bounced down the steep boulders, slick with moss, down and down, sliding inevitably toward the crashing waves below. He scrambled, trying to grab hold of something to stop his fall, but it was all too slick. He was sliding to his death.

The crab reached up with its pincher and managed to extract Merk's sword from its eye, then closed its great jaws, shattering Merk's staff into pieces. It then turned and set its sights on Merk with an eye filled with fury, a fury unlike Merk had ever seen. This crab was intent on eating him alive.

Merk, still sliding, finally grabbed hold of a nook in a rock, right before he slid off the edge. He looked down, dangling, and saw, hundreds of feet below, a plunge awaiting him into the Sea of Tears. It was a plunge that would kill him.

He looked back up and saw the crab coming down for him, somehow able to hold its balance on anything, and Merk knew he was sandwiched between two awful deaths. With death certain on either side of him, he did not know what to do.

The crab came closer, and as it was just feet away, Merk suddenly decided to choose one death over the other. Better to die by the ocean, he figured, than to be eaten alive by this thing.

Merk let go and slid down the rock, bouncing and rolling, bruising himself with every bump, sliding downward and downward. He shrieked as he fell, hardly able to catch his breath as he plummeted down, right for the ocean.

The crab, fearless, as quick as light, skittered down after him, and in one lightning fast move, it reached out with its pincher and tried to grab hold of Merk's other leg. Yet Merk was falling too fast, and to Merk's great relief, it missed.

His fall continued, until Merk suddenly came to a hard stop as he felt himself smashing into rock. He looked down, baffled, to see that, by some grace of God, there was a small stone ledge he had not seen, jutting out on the edge of the cliff, and he had luckily smashed into it. Barely wide enough to hold him, he lay there on his side, clinging to the edge of the cliff, praying for life.

The crab clearly had not expected to miss with its pincher, and the move threw it off balance: it slid over the edge, shrieking an awful high-pitched noise, and continued sliding right down the side of the cliff. As it fell it snapped its claws one last time at Merk, trying to grab him and drag him down with it, and Merk, frantic, held his breath and pulled himself in tight against the stone. It barely missed, just grazing his arm. The crab continued to fall, to his great relief, flailing, on its back, its belly exposed, its legs kicking up in the air. It dropped hundreds of feet, and Merk watched it fall, waiting, still feeling unsafe until he actually saw it dead.

The immense creature finally landed in the ocean far below, on its back, with a great cracking noise, as its shell cracked. Merk watched with great relief as it was washed away in the massive waves of the Sorrow, its

114

legs still flailing as it floated away on its back, off to some cruel and unknown death.

He lay there, on the edge of the world, and breathed deep for the first time. He looked up at the steep ascent and he could only wonder: what other horrors awaited him on the Devil's Finger?

CHAPTER TWENTY NINE

Kyra knelt on the stone as she had all night long, her legs numb, so lost in meditation that she no longer felt her body. She had slipped into a strange state where it had become hard for her to distinguish reality from fantasy, and she could no longer tell if she was awake or asleep as she slowly opened her eyes and looked out at the black sky, the million twinkling red stars, and most of all, the visage of her mother. There she was, in a flowing white robe, with startling blue eyes and long blonde hair, ascending the temple steps, approaching her, as if she had been awaiting her forever.

Kyra, breathless, studied her mother's face as she neared. It was a beautiful, timeless face, with her fine features, chiseled cheekbones, and haunting eyes, eyes that Kyra could find something of herself in. In her flowing, white gown, she seemed to float up the stairs, seemed to hover just before Kyra, just out of reach, smiling back sweetly.

"You have lost your way," her mother said, her voice so soft yet echoing throughout the empty city. It was a voice that resonated within Kyra's soul, one that she had always longed to hear. It restored her just to hear it.

"What is the way, Mother?" Kyra pleaded. "No one has ever taught me."

Her mother smiled back.

"That is because you must teach it to yourself," she replied. "The warrior does not look outward for others to train her; she looks inward. You look outward, Kyra, always, for external recognition. You search for approval, for fame, for weaponry, for teachers, for mentors. That is all an illusion, Kyra. None of them will help you. Look inside. That is the hardest journey of all."

Kyra frowned, struggling to understand.

"I…" she began, "don't know who I am, Mother."

Her mother took a deep breath. Kyra's heart pounded with anticipation as there followed a long silence, filled with nothing but the howling of the wind.

"What is it within you that you refuse to face?" her mother finally asked.

Kyra struggled with the question. As soon as her mother asked it, Kyra knew this was the question she had been grappling with all night long, the answer just out of her reach. She knew her mother was right: she was striving for approval and recognition, external ways to better herself. Her mind was so focused on the outside world, it was hard to focus internally.

116

"You must empty your mind, Kyra," her mother said. "You must unlearn everything you know."

Kyra tried, but felt she could not. Instead, she found herself distracted by a million thoughts.

"How, Mother?"

Her mother sighed.

"Stop trying to see the world for what you think it is. See it instead for what it truly is. For what it is right now, in this moment. The world right now is not what it will be a minute from now, and it is not what it was a minute ago. It is ever-changing. What do you see in the now?"

Kyra pondered her mother's question and she felt a warmth rising within her as she began to realize the truth of her mother's words. She realized she had always tried so hard to grasp onto everything, to understand it. And in that preliminary understanding, she realized now, she had lost all chance of understanding. The second she *knew* something, her knowledge was no longer true. The state she needed to strive for, she realized, was a state of continual open mind. A state of continual *not* knowing.

Kyra closed her eyes and dwelled on it. As Kyra knelt there, dwelling in her mother's meditation, she felt a warmth spreading within her, overtaking her, as she slowly felt herself filled with clarity.

After a long silence, Kyra opened her eyes, filled with understanding and excited by it.

"The true warrior," Kyra said, looking back excitedly, "knows nothing. He knows that the only battle is within one's self. The outside world is illusion."

Her mother finally smiled wide.

"Yes, my daughter."

Kyra felt the warmth continuing to spread within her, while at the same moment, the sky became filled with color. The sun began to creep over the horizon, a sliver of dawn breaking over the vast night sky. It was as if the world were waking with her. The sun and the moon hung opposite each other in the sky, the stars still between them, and Kyra knew something special was happening. She felt a power coursing through her, and for the first time, she no longer felt any lingering doubts. It was as if a veil had been lifted from the universe. Her source of power, she realized, came from her understanding.

As Kyra closed her eyes, dwelling in her enlightenment, an image flashed in her mind's eye—a baby dragon. It opened its eyes, shining, their light so intense that she gasped. She was confused to realize it was not Theos. It was a baby dragon. And far more powerful. She felt an instant connection to it.

117

She could feel its pain, its wounds, its clinging to life. And as she stared back in her mind's eye, she willed herself to heal it. To summon it.

There flashed through her mind another image: a weapon. She frowned, struggling to visualize it.

"What is it I am seeing?" Kyra asked.

There came a long silence, until finally her mother replied: "The dragon wakes. And the Staff of Truth beckons you."

"The Staff of Truth?" Kyra asked, puzzled.

"The one weapon that can save us."

Kyra, confused, tried to bring the picture into focus.

"I see it atop a mountain of ash," she said. "In a land that burns with sulfur and fire."

"It is you, Kyra," her mother said. "It is you who must go there and retrieve the weapon."

"But where?" Kyra asked. "Where is this weapon? Where must I journey?"

There came a long silence, until finally her mother uttered a single word, a word that would change her life forever:

"Marda."

CHAPTER THIRTY

The baby dragon lay on the forest floor, feeling himself dying and no longer caring. He was so weak now from loss of blood, he could barely open his eyes. He had been slipping in and out of consciousness, overwhelmed by dreams of his father coming to greet him, to escort him into a bright light.

He had fought it at first, but now he was ready to let go. This life had been too short, too painful, too confusing. He did not understand life. Why had he been born only to suffer? Why was he not meant to live longer?

Without his father alive, he felt little cause to go on. His wounds ached, but the pain lessened as he drifted more into unconsciousness, as he stopped fighting the urge to live. Death, he realized, might not be so bad after all.

As the baby was sinking, feeling more at peace, falling into a world of white, the sounds of the forest muted, distant around him, suddenly, it came. It was like a ping to his consciousness, a single direct beam of energy that startled him from his state. That brought him back.

The baby opened his eyes with a jolt and looked around, breathing hard, wondering. And then it came again.

It was real. It was a call, a command—a summons. It came from a girl in distress, a girl his father had cared for very much. A girl who was more than a girl. A human who was more than a human. It was a girl who needed him. Who was calling him. Who had a power he could not resist. A power that made him want to live.

With a new sense of purpose, the baby opened his eyes all the way and even craned his neck. He allowed the white light to fade, the feeling of comfort to fade. He embraced the pain of life, however much it hurt. After all, he was alive, and life mattered more than all. He could always die later, find peace later. But he could only live now.

The baby felt himself coursing with a new source of energy. It was a magical, mystical energy, directed by the girl, he knew, even from hundreds of miles away. It flooded his veins, gave him strength, power, reason to go on. And it healed him.

The baby sat up, reached out, and was amazed to discover that now he could extend his wings. He was even more amazed as he found himself able to flap them, to rise to his feet. He leaned back and was shocked to learn that he could even breathe fire, burning a tree before him.

The baby blinked several times, alert, alive, ready to take on the world. And as his first course of action, he ran forward, flapped his wings and leapt into the air.

Moments later he was flying, flapping, shrieking, rising higher and higher, ascending over Escalon. He flew with great speed, intent, and purpose. After all, there was a girl who needed him.

And together they would change the course of destiny.

CHAPTER THIRTY ONE

Aidan stood with Cassandra at the dungeon gate and braced himself as Pandesian soldiers closed in on them from both sides. With no possible exit, it seemed death had finally found him in his quest to free his father. Aidan prepared himself as they closed in, studying the imposing soldiers in their blue and yellow armor, and wondered which one of them would kill him first. He drew his short sword, wanting to be brave, as his father would, though he held it with trembling hands and knew it would do him no good.

"Well, it was nice knowing you," Cassandra said beside him, facing off against the soldiers, too, holding out her dagger, standing there bravely. Aidan was in awe at her composure; she showed less fear than he. She had lived a hard life on the streets, and it showed.

"I wished I could have gotten to know you," she added. "You're halfway interesting."

"Halfway?" Aidan asked.

Before she could answer, there came a noise which confused Aidan and made him turn. It was a shout—and not of Pandesians. It was a shout he recognized, a shout he had heard his entire life. A shout of his father's men.

All the Pandesian soldiers turned, too, and Aidan's heart leapt to see hundreds of his father's warriors, a manic look on their faces, bloodied, dirty, clearly having just escaped from prison, and charging right for the dungeon. They held pilfered weapons, ran with a fierce battle cry, and Aidan's heart warmed as he realized they had come for his father. They had not forgotten him.

"Let's go, boy!" yelled a voice.

Aidan turned as he felt someone yanking his arm, and he was pleasantly surprised to see Motley standing there, White at his side, pulling him away. A moment later he was off, running with Motley and Cassandra and White, all of them skirting past the Pandesian soldiers, now distracted by the large force of soldiers descending on them. Motley, with his perfect timing, as always, knew how to take advantage of distraction, and managed to lead them all away in the split-second moment of opportunity that they were afforded.

"What about the play?!" Aidan called out, breathless, as they ran through the iron gate and into the dungeons.

Motley heaved, clearly not in shape for this.

"I don't think they were enjoying it much anyway," he replied, heaving.

They all ran into the dungeon, twisting and turning their way down narrow, stone corridors, past rows of flaming torches, through open iron gates.

"Which way?" Aidan asked, looking to Motley.

Motley was barely able to catch his breath.

"You're asking me?!" he said, sprinting. "I thought I was following you!"

Suddenly, White stopped and turned, snarling. Aidan turned and was shocked to see a Pandesian soldier had broken off from the pack and had turned back for them. He sprinted after them, bearing down on them quickly.

"Stop right there!" he called out.

The soldier raised a spear, and Aidan braced himself as he knew in but a moment he would feel a spear through his back.

White snarled and leapt at the charging soldier. Aidan could not believe how fast the muscular dog closed the gap. He reached him right before he could release the spear, slamming all fours paws into his chest. He knocked him back and sank his razor-sharp fangs into the soldier's throat, killing him instantly.

White bounded off back to Aidan's side, and Aidan felt a surge of love for his dog, knowing he would be by his side forever.

The four of them continued on, running down corridors, then ducking through an arched stone passageway. They headed through another open gate, and then finally reached a crossroads, corridors leading in three different directions.

They all stopped, gasping for breath.

"Which way now?" Cassandra asked.

They all looked to Aidan and he shrugged. He knew the wrong choice would lose them the precious moments they needed and surely lead to their failure and deaths; yet he had no idea where in this vast prison complex his father could be. To his left he saw stairs going down; to his right, stairs going up.

Aidan stood there, frozen with indecision, his heart pounding. Then, finally, he decided to take a chance, praying it was the right one.

"This way," he yelled.

Aidan turned and ran to his left, down the stone stairs.

It was dark in here, and he nearly slipped on the slick surface, barely keeping his balance, taking them three at a time. The others were right behind him.

It got darker as they descended, torches lit on the walls sporadically, about every twenty feet. The stairs eventually let off at a lower level, and as Aidan hit the ground running, he found himself in a dark corridor, pathways veering left and right. He turned left, breathing hard, praying it was the right choice once again. It was too late to turn back now.

They turned down a new corridor and finally, as they turned again, they came to its end, a massive arched opening with thick iron bars. Aidan sensed this section of the dungeon, with its extra thick walls and bars, was designed to hold someone special.

Aidan charged for it. He found this gate unguarded, too, its door unlocked, and he realized all the soldiers must have been summoned up above to fight off his father's men, leaving the post vacant. He burst through and sprinted down another dark corridor until he arrived at an even darker one. He turned a corner, expecting to see his father—and was startled to find a Pandesian soldier walking right into him.

Aidan bumped into the barrel-chested soldier face first and fell to the ground. It was like hitting a wall. He looked up and saw the soldier was equally startled to see him there, too.

"Who are you?" he demanded. "What are you doing here?"

Motley, Cassandra and White caught up, and as the soldier looked at them he must have realized right away what they were up to. He drew his sword and scowled, and Aidan braced himself as he swung for him.

To Aidan's surprise, Motley lunged forward and leapt on the soldier's back, saving Aidan from a deadly blow. Motley wrestled with the bigger man awkwardly, knocking him off balance, grabbing for his arm, until finally the soldier reached around and slammed Motley into a cell.

Motley groaned and dropped to the ground, unmoving.

The soldier again set his sights on Aidan and charged for him. Aidan scurried to make it back to his feet, but knew he wouldn't make it in time—and even if he did, there would be little he could do to fend off this man. As he expected a blow in his back, suddenly Cassandra charged forward and got between him and the soldier. Aidan was in awe at her courage. She attacked the soldier, three times her size, slashing with her dagger.

But the massive soldier hardly even slowed as he merely grabbed her wrist and yanked it back. Cassandra screamed as he slammed her into a wall, sending her to the ground.

The soldier again came for Aidan, who just made his feet, and as Aidan stood there, weaponless, White lunged forward and bit down on the soldier's wrist. This soldier, though, was more tenacious than the others; while that bite would have dropped other men, this soldier merely reached around and smashed White into the wall, again and again, each blow paining Aidan to see.

White, to his credit, did not let go, yet Aidan could see he was getting badly injured.

Aidan, determined to help his friend, rushed forward and grabbed the dagger that Cassandra had dropped, raised it high, and charged. He shrieked as he sank it into the soldier's back with both hands. He felt the blade entering flesh.

The soldier shrieked this time. He immediately let go of White as he fell to the ground, then in the same motion, to Aidan's surprise, reached back and elbowed Aidan in the nose. Aidan dropped to the ground, blinded by pain. This man was a force.

The soldier turned, scowling, and somehow managed to remove the dagger from his back. In a fury, he bore down on Aidan, this time ready to kill him.

Motley, regaining his feet, rushed forward and again leapt on the soldier's back. The soldier twisted and turned, trying to knock him off, but Motley would not let go this time. In fact, he wrapped a meaty forearm around the soldier's throat, and he squeezed with all his might.

The soldier grunted and shrieked as he crisscrossed the corridor, slamming Motley into one wall after the next. Motley groaned with each slam, but to his credit, he refused to let go. The soldier simply could not manage to pry Motley's arm off his throat.

Finally, the soldier grew weak and sank to his knees.

At the same moment, Aidan raced forward, grabbed his dagger, and plunged it into the soldier's heart.

With Motley still holding his throat, the soldier dropped to the ground, dead, Motley falling on top of him.

Aidan looked over to see Motley kneeling there, covered in blood, staring down at the dead soldier as if shocked himself by what he had done.

While they all stood there, stunned, collecting themselves, Cassandra broke into action. She reached down and grabbed the keys off the soldier's waist, then ran to the final set of iron bars. She fumbled with the keys, and Aidan, realizing, hurried over and helped her, both of them trying one after the next.

Finally, there came a click and they swung the cell door open.

They burst into the final, darkened cell, even darker than the others. As they raced through it, colder in here, more damp, Aidan wondered how any human being could keep anyone down here. It was too cruel for words.

"FATHER!" Aidan called out, hoping, praying.

Aidan ran through the dark room, unable to see his feet, stumbling, lit only by a single torch in the far corner. He prayed he had found the right place; after all, this was the lowest cell in the lowest part of the dungeon complex, and it seemed to him the logical place to keep their most important prisoner. If not, there would be no turning back—he would fail his father, and they would all die down here.

"FATHER!" he shrieked again, running desperately through the cavernous room, fanning out with the others. He was beginning to lose hope. Had he been crazy to attempt to come down here in the first place?

124

"Aidan?" came a weak voice.

It was so weak that Aidan at first wondered if he had heard it. Then he felt his heart rise into his throat as he detected motion in the darkness.

He rushed to the far wall, and there, barely illuminated in the dark cell, was his father. Aidan wept at the sight of him. There sat his father, a broken man, emaciated, shackled to the floor like an animal, too weak to sit up. He had never seen him like this and it broke his heart.

"Father!"

Aidan rushed to his father's side, knelt down, and hugged him. His father, in shackles, was barely able to hug him back, but he did as much as he could. Aidan was brimming with joy; it had been such a long journey since setting out from Volis, a journey he had never thought he would actually complete.

"Aidan," his father replied weakly. His father seemed stunned, as if Aidan were the last person he had expected to see. "What are you doing here? Why are you not in Volis?"

His father looked over and peered at Motley, Cassandra and White as they closed in.

"And who are these people with you?"

Aidan's heart fell to see the sorry state his father was in, his chapped lips and bruised body. He could only imagine what they had done to him.

He held out his water sack, and his father drank greedily.

"Not too much," Motley cautioned, stepping forward, holding the sack. "He will get sick."

Aidan pulled back the sack as his father gasped with a great breath of relief.

"The keys!" Aidan called out, pained to see his father in shackles.

Cassandra rushed forward and fumbled with the key ring until she finally unlocked the shackles securing Duncan's wrists and ankles.

His father leaned forward and fell into Aidan's arms, too weak to stand. They all helped him to his feet, and Motley draped an arm around his shoulder, helping him to stand, to walk.

Distant noises of conflict erupted somewhere above ground.

"We must go!" Motley urged.

They hobbled back down through the dungeon corridors, past all the other cells, turning down endless halls. Aidan could hardly believe he actually had his father in his arms, that he really did it. Seeing him, he felt a reason to live again.

They turned down one corridor after another, until they finally reached the staircase again. They climbed the steps as best they could, all dragging Duncan, until finally they reached the upper level.

It was brighter up here, and Aidan, glad to smell fresh air again, could hear the fighting in the distance. He saw his father's men, still locked in battle with the Pandesian soldiers. His father's men, he was dismayed to see, were surrounded, many of them falling. Yet they were not backing down, and they were providing the crucial distraction that Aidan needed.

Aidan ran in their direction, sticking to the shadows, to any recesses in the wall they could find. His heart slammed as they made their way down the corridors, getting ever closer to the exit, to freedom. He craved to be back on the streets, far away from this place, from Andros, yet he had a sinking feeling he would never get out of here alive.

Finally, as they turned down the final corridor, Aidan saw it, right there before them: the door to freedom. It was open.

Aidan stepped out of the shadows, preparing to run for it, when suddenly, his view went black. He looked up to see his path was blocked. Standing before them was a huge Pandesian soldier, holding a sword and blocking their way.

"And just where do you think you're going?" he sneered, looking over the group of them, his eyes resting on Duncan.

The soldier stepped forward, sword raised high, and Aidan knew they were finished. With Duncan in tow, there was no way they could defend themselves, and none of them were well armed enough, or could react quickly enough, to stop this man. Aidan braced himself for a sword in his gut. Even worse, for his father to be killed. What an awful place to die, he thought. Right here, just when they were staring at the gates to freedom.

Suddenly, the soldier gasped and dropped to his knees, falling face first in front of them, dead.

Aidan looked down, shocked, seeing a hatchet in his back.

He looked up and was baffled to see another Pandesian soldier approaching to kill them. He was confused. Why, he wondered, would a Pandesian soldier kill one of his own?

Aidan braced himself as the other Pandesian neared.

But then the Pandesian raised his helmet, revealing himself, and Aidan's heart flooded with shock as he saw who it was:

Anvin.

"Anvin!" Duncan cried, seeing his old friend.

Anvin rushed forward and embraced them all, and without hesitating draped an arm around Duncan, helping to prop him up.

"We must hurry!"

Aidan saw a boy about his age come running forward, in a panic, and as he ran to Anvin's side and began to help carry Duncan, he realized it must be Anvin's squire.

The group of them turned and burst out of the final cell, out of the dungeons, back into the streets, and somewhere, in the chaotic capital night,   toward   freedom.

CHAPTER THIRTY TWO

Merk hiked along the endless rocks of the Devil's Finger, slipping, struggling to keep his footing, nearly drunk with exhaustion as he headed into the sunset. His eyes were so heavy he could barely keep them open, and he ached from every corner of his body, most of all from the wound left by that crab, still festering on his shin. Yet he knew he was lucky to be alive.

Endless waves of fog rolled in, carried by gusts of wind off the ocean and bay, some strong enough to knock him off balance. All the while he was plagued by the distant sound of the horns of Marda, echoing in the fog, haunting him, keeping the pressure on. After so many days of hiking without another soul in sight, he was beginning to realize why no one else dared this: hiking the Devil's Finger meant taking your life into your hands.

Merk was losing hope of ever reaching the Tower of Kos; he was beginning to wonder if it truly existed, or if it was just a legend. He felt so weak, hands trembling from exhaustion, he knew he could never make it back. He found himself fantasizing about life on the mainland, about the bounties of Escalon. What he would give to be on flat, smooth, dry land again. To be anywhere in the world but here.

Each step more and more of an effort, Merk found himself sinking into despair. He caught himself looking down into the cracks and wondering how easy it might be to just step inside one of them and allow himself to plummet to his death. He looked left and right, to the ocean and to the bay, and realized how easy it would be to allow himself to slip over the edge, to plummet to his death. Maybe, he started to think, it would be a relief.

Merk looked up, hopeful despite himself one last time as he mounted another boulder—yet was crushed to see nothing but more rocks. He was certain that this was what death felt like, an endless trek to nowhere, tortured with each step. This was payback for the life he had led. After all, he had murdered dozens of people in his life, for hire, and this lonely hike forced him to reflect on all of them. He saw their faces, thought of the life he had led honestly for the first time, and he did not like what he saw. This odyssey, strangely enough, had been the *true* pilgrimage for him. Maybe that's why the Sword of Fire was here.

If Merk had hoped to repent and reflect, he could not have hoped for a better place. Day after day of hiking these rocky cliffs, of not seeing a soul, of being engulfed in mist and fog, each step nearly slipping to his death, forced Merk to appreciate life. He wanted, for the first time, to *live*, to truly live. He wanted a chance to start life anew.

As the hours passed, the sun falling, Merk heard a noise, felt something on his cheeks, and he realized he was weeping. He was startled, and had no idea why. As he reflected, he realized it was a cry of regret, regret for the life he had lived. Regret for not being able to take it all back, to try again. He desperately wished to do it all differently, to have just one more chance.

Another gust of wind ripped through, and as the fog lifted, the sun, for the first time, shone down. Merk looked up and this time, he stopped, standing there in shock. His breath caught in his throat as he stared into the distance.

There, on the horizon, was a rainbow. He was not sure if he had ever believed in God, but this time, he felt God was answering him. He felt he was being offered redemption. He stopped and stood there and wept uncontrollably, not understanding life. He felt a part of him had died along the way and a new part was sprouting.

As Merk looked out beyond it, he saw another sight, one which stirred within him an even more intense mixture of feeling. The Sea of Sorrow met the Bay of Death. The two bodies of water conjoined, swirling with foam. The peninsula came to an end. The seas were shining. And standing there amidst all that light, Merk was amazed and elated to see, was a single structure.

A tower.

There it was, the ancient Tower of Kos, rising up in that landscape, amidst all the nothingness, as if emerging from the very stone itself. There it stood, perched proudly at the end of the world.

The Tower of Kos was real. And it stood right before him.

*

Merk scrambled down the last boulder, landing on gravel and sighing with relief. He had never been so grateful to be on dry, flat land. He could walk again, quickly and steadily, with no fear of falling. His boots crunched gravel and he had never enjoyed the feeling as much.

The Tower of Kos stood right before him, hardly fifty feet away, and Merk looked up and studied it in awe. Behind it the waves of the ocean and bay intersected and crashed, offering a stunning backdrop. As he looked up at the tower, what surprised Merk most was that he had seen it before; it appeared to be an exact replica of the Tower of Ur. The stone, the height, the diameter—each seemed to have been constructed at the same time, mysteriously, at opposite corners of the kingdom. But how? Merk wondered. How could one even manage to construct anything out here, at the edge of the world?

Merk stared up at the shining golden doors, just like the doors of Ur, and as he looked closely, he did notice a small difference: these doors bore a different insignia than the doors of Ur, were carved with different symbols, images. He wished now, more than ever, that he could read. What did it all mean? There was an image of a long sword, flames surrounding it, carved into the gold. It dominated both doors and crossed over them, placed horizontally.

As Merk stood there, he sensed a different energy to this tower. He could not put his finger on it, but something felt off. It was an *absence*. Oddly, it felt as if this place were abandoned.

Merk stepped forward, closer, and as he did, he was even more shocked to find the doors ajar. He felt a chill up his spine. How could the doors to the scared Tower of Kos lie open? Unguarded? Had someone beaten him here? What could it all mean?

Merk stepped closer, on edge, no longer knowing what to expect, and as he did, to his even greater shock, the doors began to open. Perplexed, he stood there, as out of the blackness there emerged a person. Not just any person—but the most beautiful girl he had ever seen. It made no sense. It was like an apparition.

With so many shocking things happening at once, Merk could not process it all. He did not know what he was most amazed by. He was speechless as this woman stood before the doors, staring back at him with her translucent blue eyes, her stunning features, perhaps in her twenties. Even stranger, he had the crazy feeling that he knew her, that he recognized her from somewhere. He recalled all his years of serving the old King Tarnis and as he looked at her, with her glowing blue eyes, her silvery-blonde hair, he could not help but think that she looked exactly like the old King Tarnis.

It made no sense. How could it be? Tarnis, as far as he knew, never had a daughter.

Or did he?

She stood there, looking back with such grace, such poise, he couldn't see how she could be anything but royalty. Yet there was something more to her. Her face was so white, nearly translucent, radiating an intense energy, as if she were not entirely human. The last time he had felt this way was in the presence of a Watcher.

She stood there in the silence, punctuated by nothing but the wind and the waves, and as much as he wanted to know more, he also felt an urgency to get to the heart of the matter, to begin preparations to alert her, to protect the Sword, given the trolls were hardly a day behind him.

"My lady," he began, "I have come on an urgent mission. An army advances here, an army of trolls, bent on destruction. They have come to kill you and everyone here, and to take the Sword."

As she stared back, he was surprised to see no reaction—no fear, nothing. She remained expressionless. Perhaps she did not believe him. He wondered at his state, at what he might look like after that hike, and realized he could hardly blame her. Maybe in her eyes he was just a madman appearing out of the fog.

"I know that the Sword resides here," he continued, determined. "I served at the Tower of Ur—the tower which is no more."

Again, he searched her face for a reaction—and again, to his confusion, there came none.

"There is no time, my lady," he urged. "We must secure the Sword before they arrive. We must prepare a defense immediately."

He expected her to be dismayed, panic-stricken, but to his great surprise, she stood there with a slight smile at the corners of her lips, completely unfazed, holding more poise than anyone he'd ever seen.

"Is this not news that I bring you?" he finally asked, baffled.

"It is not," she replied, her voice so smooth, so peaceful, it completely threw him off guard.

He was stunned.

"But how could you know all this?" he asked. "And if you knew all this…" he said, struggling to understand, "then…why are you still here? Why haven't you fled?"

"Only I remain," she replied patiently. "I sent the others away, long ago, the day that Marda crossed into Ur."

Merk stared back, shocked. He looked up at the empty tower in wonder.

"Are you saying that you are here alone?" he asked. "Why have you not fled yourself?"

She smiled.

"Because I was waiting for you," she replied flatly.

"For *me*?!" he asked, flabbergasted.

"I was waiting to save you," she added.

He didn't know what to say. Was she mocking him?

"But I have come here to save *you*," he countered.

Merk stood there, anxiety rising within him as heard, yet again, the sound of the troll army in the distance.

"Who are you?" he asked, burning with curiosity.

But she would not reply. Merk was increasingly agitated.

"I do not understand," he said. "We have no time. If there is no one here, we must secure the Sword, take it far from here and leave this place."

Still, she did not react.

"Tell me," he insisted, desperate, wondering if he had made this long trek for nothing. "Is the Sword of Fire still here?"

To his surprise, she answered simply.

"Yes."

His eyes widened. The Sword of Fire. The Sword of legend, which had haunted his dreams his entire life. It really existed. And it lay just beyond those doors.

"Then we must save it!" he said, and began to walk for the doors.

She blocked his way, and he stared back, puzzled.

"Do you really think a man could save the Sword?" she asked.

He stared back, confused.

"Perhaps the Sword is not meant to be saved," she added.

He struggled to understand.

"What do you mean?" he asked, frustrated. "It is meant to be guarded. That is the purpose we serve."

She nodded.

"Guarded, yes," she said. "But not saved. The Sword has been guarded for centuries. Yet when the time comes for it to be taken away, it is not for us to interfere with destiny. The Sword has its own destiny, and that, no man can alter."

Merk stood there, uncomprehending.

"If you don't believe me, then try," she said.

She stepped aside and motioned at the open doors behind her. He looked past her and saw a faint torchlight beckoning.

Merk glanced back over his shoulder and saw, on the horizon, the nation of Marda getting closer with each step. He turned back to the tower, feeling a need to do something.

Merk broke into action. He rushed past her and inside the tower, entering the blackened chamber. He stood inside, where it was cool and quiet, the crashing of the waves and howling of the wind muted for the first time in his long journey. He turned about slowly, his eyes adjusting to the darkness, and with a jolt of shock he saw, sitting there, just a few feet away, what could only be the Sword of Fire.

There it sat, glowing red, right in the center of the chamber, on a pedestal, in plain sight. Merk could not understand why it was not hidden.

Following a gut impulse to save it, Merk ran forward, reached out, and without hesitating, grabbed hold of its hilt, determined to take it away somewhere safe.

Merk heard a hissing noise and felt a burning in his palm unlike any he had ever felt. His hand burned as the hilt seared his skin. He shrieked, pulling back his hand, and as he did, he saw the damage it had left: the insignia of the Sword burned into his palm.

He stood there, in tears from the pain, holding his smoldering hand.

"I warned you," came the soft voice.

Merk turned to see the girl standing beside him. He knew then that she was right; everything she had said had been right.

131

"So what do we do?" he asked, clutching his arm, feeling helpless.

"A ship awaits," she said. "Come with me."

She held out a hand, long and pale, and he stood there, debating. She was inviting him to leave this place, to leave the Sword behind, to journey to some other place he would not know. He knew that taking her hand would change his life forever, would put him a road from which there would be no return. Would leave the Sword here, all alone, at the mercy of its enemies.

But maybe that was what was meant to be. The laws of destiny, after all, were beyond him.

Merk stared into those translucent eyes, at her open palm, so inviting, and he knew his mind was already made up.

He reached out and took it, and as he did, he knew his life would never be the same again.

CHAPTER THIRTY THREE

Vesuvius, finally reaching the end of the Devil's Finger, leapt down from the last boulder onto dry land, his boots crunching on gravel, and felt a wave of relief. There he stood, defiant amidst the raging wind and crashing seas, and looked up, salivating at his destination: the Tower of Kos. He felt a warmth tingling up his arms, and he could not stop himself from grinning. He had really made it. In but minutes, the Sword would be his.

Behind him came the clattering of thousands of soldiers, his nation of trolls scrambling down off the boulders, landing on the gravel. They stood behind him, awaiting his command, all ready to march to their deaths on a moment's notice.

Vesuvius stood there in silence punctuated only by the wind, reveling in the moment. He had crossed all of Escalon for this; now, finally, there was nothing left to stand in his way, to stand between he and the Sword of Fire, between him and his destiny. Soon the Sword would be his, the Flames would be a memory, and the entire nation of Marda would advance. Escalon would be forgotten, and renamed Greater Marda.

Vesuvius marched forward, his trolls following close behind, each step bringing him closer to those magnificent golden doors, shining in the last rays of sun. They were ajar, he was surprised to see, and this place, he realized, had the feeling of being abandoned. For a moment he felt a pang of fear. Had they all left? Had they taken the Sword with them?

Or, worse—had it never been here to begin with?

Vesuvius reached the doors and yanked them open all the way, heart pounding, dozens of trolls rushing forward to help. He did not need their help. With a single hand, with his massive strength, he yanked the heavy doors open all the way, as determined to enter as he had ever had been to do anything in his life.

Vesuvius crossed the threshold. It was dark in here, the sound of the wind and the waves muted, and he heard only the crackling of torches inside. It was cooler in here, too. He stepped forward, feeling his destiny rise up within him.

He stopped as his eyes adjusted, and held his breath. He could not believe his eyes: there it sat, before him, the Sword of Fire. It was glowing, as if aflame, a beautiful sword, perhaps three feet long, with the hilt shining yellow, and the blade flaming orange. The blade stuck straight up, pointing to the ceiling.

Vesuvius's heart slammed in his chest. Finally. There it was, after all this. The source of his years of tireless work. Of his father's and his father's before him. Now here he stood, just feet away from it. It seemed too good to be true. As if, perhaps, it were a trick.

Vesuvius rushed forward, his palms sweaty, unable to wait a moment longer. He stood beside the sword, sweating, examining it, feeling its heat from here. It was a thing of beauty. A thing of majesty. It even emanated a sound of its own, like the sound of a hissing torch. It seemed primal, like one of the wonders of the earth.

Vesuvius, unable to wait any longer, reached out and grabbed the hilt, ready for his entire life to change.

Immediately, he was blinded by pain. He shrieked and shrieked as the hilt seared his palm, burning into it, deeper and deeper as he gripped it, the pain more intense than anything he had ever felt. He desperately wanted to let go, every nerve within him screamed at him to let go, but he forced himself to hang on as long as he could stand it. He knew if he let it go he would never touch it again. And he could not give up. Not now. Not after all this.

Yet, shrieking, sweating, his palm sizzling, smoking, the pain was too intense even for him.

Vesuvius finally had no choice but to release his grip on the hilt and back away, holding his wrist in agony. He looked down at his hand and saw the insignia of the hilt burned into his palm forever.

He turned, scowling at his trolls, who looked back at him, all terrified to come near him.

"You," he spat to one nameless troll, as he held his wrist, gasping in pain.

The troll stepped forward.

"Grab the Sword!"

Vesuvius knew from legend that the Sword needed to leave the tower for the Flames to lower.

"Me, my lord?" asked the troll, terror-stricken.

Vesuvius rushed forward, shrieking, drew his sword with his good hand, and stabbed the hesitating troll in the heart.

He then turned to his other trolls.

"You!" he said to another, pointing at him with the tip of his sword.

The troll gulped. He stepped forward reluctantly and made his way toward the Sword. Sweating, he hesitated, looking over at Vesuvius.

Vesuvius's unyielding glare must have convinced the vacillating troll. He stepped forward, and with trembling hands reached out and grabbed the hilt of the Sword.

The soldier shrieked as he did, his hands burning—and before he could remove his grip, Vesuvius ran up behind him, wrapped one arm around his throat from behind in a chokehold, and reached down and grabbed the man's hand with his good hand. He squeezed as tight as he could, forcing the troll not to let go of the Sword.

The troll shrieked, clearly in agony, yet Vesuvius held him firmly in place, squeezing the life out of him.

"HELP!" Vesuvius shrieked.

The other trolls rushed forward and helped him, grabbing the troll's wrist and arm, forcing him to hold on.

"PULL!" Vesuvius commanded.

As one, all held tightly to the soldier and yanked him back, shrieking all the while.

Vesuvius couldn't stand the noise anymore—annoyed, he tightened his chokehold, then with a quick, simple move, snapped the troll's neck. The troll hung limply in his arms, Vesuvius's other hand still clamping the dead troll's hand on the Sword.

Together, they all dragged the dead troll out the door, and out of the tower, the Sword still in his hand.

The second they crossed the threshold of the tower, the second they stepped outside, Vesuvius sensed something happening. Even though it was hundreds of miles away, he could feel it from here.

The Flames. They were beginning to weaken.

"TO THE SEA!" Vesuvius shrieked.

The trolls joined him as they dragged the limp troll, the Sword still clamped in his hand, toward the edge of the cliff. As they reached it, Vesuvius picked up the dead soldier high overhead, clamping his hand over the Sword hand, then rushed forward and hurled him over the cliff.

Vesuvius leaned over and watched, his heart pounding with excitement, as the limp troll went flying over the cliff, hurtling toward the ocean below, the Sword still in his hand. The Sword fell with him, finally separating from his hand halfway, tumbling end over end. As it fell through the air, Vesuvius was amazed to watch it morph into a ball of flame, like a comet falling from the sky.

Finally it hit the sea, and as it impacted the water there followed an enormous explosion, the likes of which Vesuvius had never seen. A column of water, turned orange, shot up into the sky, hundreds of feet high, then showered down all around him, its waters scalding, like drops of fire.

The world shook beneath his feet, and he felt it happening.

The Flames were no more.

He grinned wide, realizing.

Escalon   was   his.

CHAPTER THIRTY FOUR

Alec sat before the forge, sweating, hammering away at the sword as he had been for days, frustrated and stumped. This unfinished sword, crafted of a metal he did not understand, just would not mold. It was the most stubborn piece of metal he had ever worked with. Try as he did to shape it, the sword seemed to have a mind of its own. He had tried softening it with liquid fire, cooling it, and hammering it from every angle, with every type of hammer. Nothing worked.

Alec sat there, shoulders aching, and put his hammer down, needing a break. He examined it, breathing hard, dripping sweat onto it, and wondered. He held it up to the light, palms raw from hammering, and turned it, trying to understand. He had never encountered anything remotely like it. It was half a sword, an unfinished masterpiece of a weapon that refused to be finished, a weapon as mysterious as any he had ever held. He understood now why these islanders needed him here, on the Lost Isles, to complete it. It seemed he was set up for an impossible task.

Alec finally threw his hammer down in frustration, the hammer echoing on the floor. He sat there, head in his hands, trying to think. He hated being defeated.

He stared back at the sword and he could feel its energy, even from here, coming at him in waves, as if taunting him. It was like sharing the room with another person. He felt the sword craved attention, and he studied it, unable to look away. It was stubborn, proud, magical. He ran his hand along its too-sharp blade; he felt the jagged end, where the blade was unfinished, turned it over and studied the strange inscriptions. It bore ancient symbols he did not understand, like a riddle that needed to be cracked.

Alec wondered what it all could mean. Who had forged this? When? Why hadn't they finished it? Had they been interrupted? Or was it unfinished on purpose? Had it been broken in battle? If so, by what weapon? Was there a matching sword somewhere, one that was complete? If so, where was it?

Most of all, why could it not be forged? What was it made of? What did he have to do to finish it?

Alec felt the answer lying right before him, just out of his reach. It was a riddle, this sword, one that would not let him think of anything else. He had to solve it.

Yet he had no idea how. He was dealing with something here that was clearly not of this earth, that was way out of his element. With any other weapon, he would know exactly what to do. If nothing else, he could simply start from scratch. But not this one. He examined its exotic material, turning it over as it shined in the light, and wondered what it was. It had a light blue sheen, and the more he stared at it, the more it seemed to change. It was like staring into the endless waters of a lake. What was the purpose of this weapon? he wondered. Why was it needed so desperately? How could it impact all of Escalon?

Alec finally, exhausted, set it down. He wiped sweat off his forehead and stood, stretching his aching limbs. He sighed. Maybe they had been wrong about him. Maybe he wasn't the one meant to finish it.

Alec, brooding, stormed out of the forge and emerged into the foggy sunlight, squinting, trying to adjust. A dramatic sunset cast a scarlet light over the Lost Isles, and everywhere sunlight sparkled in a silver mist. This place was magical.

Alec decided to take a walk. He paced on the strange terrain, soft green moss beneath his boots, and he looked out and studied the sky, the landscape, breathing in the fresh ocean air. He struggled, dwelling on the sword as he hiked. What did its inscriptions mean? Why was it unfinished?

Alec walked for hours, as the sunset mysteriously lingered, never seeming to set. Here, in the Lost Isles, he had learned that it never really grew dark; this eerie sunset lingered all night long, never quite dark, allowing just enough light for him to walk by.

As he hiked and studied the landscape, he climbed a hill and noticed something in the distance for the first time. Against the silhouette of the dying sun he spotted a massive boulder, tall and skinny, set high on a hill. The more he examined it, the more it began to dawn on him: the unusual shape of the boulder. It shot straight up, tall and skinny, and it seemed to have no end. It was jagged. It seemed...unfinished.

He was flooded with excitement as he realized: the boulder had the exact shape of the sword.

Alec ran toward the boulder, and as he reached it, he stopped and, breathing hard, laid both hands on the stone. He felt it, and was amazed by its intense energy, amazed that it was cool to the touch, just like the sword. His heart quickened as he looked up and studied it, wondering. Could the sword have been crafted of this same material?

Alec drew the spare chisel from his belt, raised it, and on a hunch, hit the stone with all he could. The stone chipped, and he was thrilled to see, beneath it, a material of sparkling blue. This was it, Alec realized. The material from which the sword was forged.

Alec hammered away at it, hoping to be able to remove a chunk, to take it back, to complete the sword; yet as he reached the inside layers, as his hammer met the blue material, the stone would not give. It was as stubborn and un-malleable as the sword. Alec stood there, crestfallen, realizing he had reached a dead end.

137

Suddenly, the ground trembled beneath his feet and a loud hissing noise cut through the air. Alec looked up, beyond the rock, and was astounded to see a sight he had never thought to see in his life. There, beyond the boulder, was a huge mountain, and at its top, bright-red lava began to squirt forth amidst great plumes of smoke. It was a volcano. And it was beginning to erupt.

Alec looked down at the boulder before him, then back to the volcano, and he suddenly realized: this boulder had emerged from the lava, from some ancient spewing forth of the volcano. It was the volcano that had forged it, that was the source of all the power on this island. That which was most malleable became that which was un-malleable.

Alec, breathless with excitement, turned and sprinted back to the dwelling housing the sword. He snatched it and turned and ran back through the landscape, breathless, until he returned to the volcano. He sprinted up the hill, hardly pausing, lungs aching but carried on by his adrenaline. He did not even pause to consider how dangerous it was to be scaling an active volcano, even as the heat and smoke began to make the sweat pour down his face. He scaled the side where lava was not spewing forth, and hoped and prayed the lava did not change course.

Alec finally reached the top of the volcano, and he stopped at its edge and looked down, shocked. There, below, was an active, bubbling volcano, its red and white lava swirling far below, molten hot. He could barely see from the smoke and barely breathe from the heat. Yet as he stood there, he felt the sword vibrating in his hands, and he knew: this was the place the sword was meant to be. This was what the sword needed to complete it.

Alec, sweat pouring off him, knew he could not survive up here much longer. He felt the sword shaking now, and he knew he had to do something fast. He searched his belt and extracted the long chain he kept, and slowly unraveled it. He quickly tied one end to the hilt, and then, following his instinct, he dropped the sword over the edge, held the chain tight, and slowly lowered it.

Alec lowered the chain link one foot at a time, quickly losing sight of the sword amidst the smoke and heat. He pulled his face back from the edge, recoiling as a blast of heat nearly seared his skin, and he continued to lower the sword, his hands nearly burning from the heat on the steel.

As he reached the final link, Alec looked over. Far below, amidst the smoke, he barely caught a glimpse of the sword. It hung, swinging on the chain, a good thirty feet below, its unfinished end pointing down as burst of lava shot up toward it. And as he watched, the strangest thing happened. It seemed as if the lava were redirecting itself, bursting and gathering around the tip of the blade.

Alec suddenly felt the chain tugging at him, as if he had a shark on the other end of the line, and it took all his might just to hold on. He wondered what was happening. Was this madness? Would he lose the sword?

Finally, the resistance stopped and the chain went slack.

Sweating, frantic, Alec pulled back at the chain, yanking it as fast as he could go. He pulled it up faster and faster, not feeling anything, desperate that he might have lost it.

As he finished pulling the chain and reached its end, and his worst fears were confirmed: there was nothing on the end of it. He had lost the sword.

Alec sat there, staring, blinking, frozen in despair, unable to move. He had lost the sword. The last hope for Escalon. He had failed all these people on a mad whim, had let them all down.

Suddenly there arose a great rumble, and Alec stumbled as the ground beneath him shook. Lava began to shoot out from the volcano in all directions, and as a glob of it scorched Alec's arm, he realized he had no choice. He had to flee if he had any hope of survival.

Alec turned and fled down the mountain, and as he reached its base, he stopped and watched, raising a hand to his eyes. The volcano shook and finally, amidst plumes of smoke, it exploded.

Fountains of lava burst forth in all directions, and amidst them, shooting up in the sky, was a sight that Alec would never forget: the sword. It flew up into the air, soared in a great arc, and then, turning end over end, it landed in the soft dirt before Alec, just feet away, as if awaiting him.

It sat there, its blade embedded in the ground, still swaying.

And Alec's heart stopped as he saw it, gleaming, nearly as tall as he.

The   sword   of   swords   was   complete.

CHAPTER THIRTY FIVE

Dierdre and Marco sprinted through the war-torn streets of Ur, narrowly avoiding the collapse of yet another building, smashed by a cannonball, as it crumbled behind them. Dierdre held a hand to her face as she ran through a massive cloud of dust, coughing, trying to catch her breath, while all around them ancient buildings collapsed and the city was reduced to mountains of rubble. Cannon fire echoed throughout the city as the Pandesians unleashed volley after volley, and Dierdre found herself stumbling over bodies, old, young, men, women, children, some faces whom she recognized. All the people of Ur, it seemed, were now dead.

The city was becoming a massive tomb, as an endless stream of Pandesian soldiers disembarked from the ships and stormed it on foot, butchering any survivors. The only thing keeping Dierdre and Marco alive while running was the massive cloud of dust that kept them obscured. Dierdre's heart slammed as she sprinted, wondering if this would ever end.

She felt a strong grip on her wrist, and she turned to see Marco yanking her down a side street, then behind the safety of a pile of rubble. It was just in time; a dozen Pandesian soldiers raced past, spears out in front, looking for blood. She watched as they went from body to body lying on the stone, some of them moaning, and stabbed each one, putting spears into their hearts to make sure they were dead.

Dierdre nearly gagged. She looked out ahead and saw the occasional survivor still running through the streets, hunted down like prey as soldiers descended on them like a pack of wolves. Dierdre's veins coursed with indignation; she was desperate for vengeance. She knew it was madness to be up on these streets, that if she wanted any chance of survival, she should have stayed down below, in the safety of the tunnels, with the rest of the citizens she had saved. Yet, safety was not what she wanted. She wanted to die on her feet, inflicting as much damage as she could while facing the enemy proudly.

Dierdre thought of her dead father, seeing his face in death, and the anger overtook her once again. She needed to avenge him. She recalled how she herself had been treated by the Pandesians, her captivity, and she knew that vengeance had been a long time coming. For her, it was not even a choice. It had become all she had left to live for.

Dierdre looked about at all the devastation, and realized how stupid she had been to think they could defend this place. She remembered how hard they had all worked to forge weapons, to prepare, how futile that had been. She wondered again how Alec could have abandoned them. She was disappointed, embarrassed that she had ever had faith in him. How could he have fled all his friends in such a cowardly way?

Dierdre tried to focus, remembering her reason for surfacing: the chains. Alec's unfinished work. If she and Marco could just affix one chain, take out just one Pandesian ship, they could kill hundreds. That would be enough for her. It would give her the satisfaction she desperately required, and she could die happily after that.

She turned and studied the canals. Through the rising dust, she spotted what they had come for: one of the places where they had laid chains before the invasion. They had been preparing when they had been all caught off guard by the sudden invasion. All the chains still lay there, unused, none having a chance to even be affixed to the canals below.

"There!" she called to Marco, pointing.

Marco turned to look, and he nodded back knowingly.

Dierdre looked toward the sea and saw a towering Pandesian warship sailing into the canal. She could barely make it out in the haze, about fifty yards away and closing in fast, and she knew there was little time.

Marco turned and looked at her, sweating, fear in his face, and nodded back.

"Okay," he said, "let's do it."

They held hands, squeezing them tightly, and took off. They jumped up and ran through the clouds of dust, weaving out of the way of roving packs of Pandesian soldiers, of collapsing walls, Dierdre wondering if they would even reach the edge of the canal, just thirty feet away. Dierdre could not help but notice the strength and assurance she felt in Marco's presence. She felt an even stronger connection with him than she'd had with Alec, this boy who had cared enough to stay behind and help her.

They finally reached the edge, and as they did, Dierdre jumped onto her stomach, avoiding a spear sailing through the air. Marco dropped beside her, then jumped into the canal, and he grabbed her hand and dragged her down with him.

Dierdre felt a shock as she was submerged in the icy water up to her waist. She grabbed hold of the slimy stone wall and stood on a stone ledge about four feet deep, up against it. She closed her eyes, not wanting to look at all the corpses floating by on their backs, eyes up, looking to the heavens as if wondering how this could have happened.

"I'll cross to the other side!" Marco said. "You stay here!"

He pushed off the wall, making his way across the canal, and as he swam, Dierdre caught her breath and yelled: "Marco!"

A spear sailed through the air, just missing him, plunging into the water. She turned and looked up and saw a lone Pandesian soldier running alongside the canal, looking down at them. She braced herself as he spotted her and raised an arm to throw another spear at her.

There came a sudden explosion, and another cloud of dust rolled through, obscuring the soldier. Dierdre held her breath and plunged underwater. She looked up, through the water, for as long as she could, until she watched him, impatient, search the waters, then run on to another, easier, target.

Dierdre surfaced, gasping, then turned and looked anxiously to see if Marco had surfaced at the other end. Finally, she spotted him also surfacing, dripping wet, and she breathed a sigh of relief.

Marco reached up, grabbed the heavy chain from the far side of the canal, and dragged it down into the water with him. He tried to affix it to the huge iron hooks at the far side of the canal, but he struggled with it, trying to raise it and failing several times.

There came a horn and Dierdre turned and looked up the canal to see the hull of the massive ship bearing down on her. She knew they had no time.

Come on, Marco! she willed.

Finally, he lifted the heavy iron with shaking hands and hooked the chain into place.

Dierdre swam over to her end of the chain, grabbed hold of it, still dangling at the edge, and raised it with all her might, trying to attach it. It was too much for her to lift, her arms shaking with the effort, and unable to do it, she slid back down.

She closed her eyes, and she saw her father's face. Breathing hard, she willed herself to be stronger.

Come on. You can do this. For your father. For yourself.

Dierdre thought of every injustice she had ever received at the hand of the Pandesians, and she finally opened her eyes, let out a great shriek, and with all her might, lifted the chain again. This time it went a few inches higher, just enough so that she could affix it on the hook. She dropped it and it landed with satisfying clink.

She breathed with relief, gulping hard, and turned and looked across the canal. She saw the chain, taut, stretching from one side to the other, all the spikes near the surface, ready. She grabbed the crank beside the hook, as did Marco, each of them waiting. They looked at each other, then turned and watched the oncoming Pandesian warship, now but twenty feet away. They waited, watching silently, Dierdre's heart pounding.

The ship came closer and closer, until finally it was so close that Dierdre could see the barnacles attached to its hull. Marco turned and nodded at her, and she nodded back. The time had come.

They each turned their cranks at the same time, and as they did, Dierdre felt the chain become more taut. It rose just above the surface, its spikes protruding, and she watched in satisfaction as the ship bore down on it, but feet away, too late to stop.

Dierdre suddenly scrambled up and out of the canal, as did Marco, and she dove to the cobblestone streets just as the ship smashed into the spikes.

There came a tremendous cracking noise, and she watched with glee as the massive vessel began to crack, and then splinter.

Within moments, the entire ship was buckling, caving in.

Soldiers shrieked as they realized. They stumbled and then, as they looked over the edge to see what was happening, fell over the sides. They scrambled about in confusion, trying to stop the ship, to turn it back, but there was no time. The ship continued to sail into the spikes, and within moments it collapsed into a pile of wood.

All the soldiers shrieked as they were thrown overboard, all unable to swim in their armor, sinking into the depths as fast as their ship.

Dierdre looked across the harbor to see Marco smiling back at her, and she knew they had done it. Their deaths might be imminent, but at least they'd had their moment of revenge. They'd shown the Pandesians that they could be hurt, that Ur could fight back.

Horns sounded all up and down the harbor, and Dierdre turned to see other Pandesian ships take notice of what had happened. They all suddenly stopped in the harbor before entering the canals. And then, as she watched them, they all began to do something even more curious—they began to turn around and sail back into the harbor, away from Ur.

It was strange. Why, she wondered, were they leaving? It was as if they all wanted to get as far away as possible. But why?

A chorus of horns suddenly sounded, and on their heels there followed a cacophony of cannon fire. The air shook and thunder filled the city, and Dierdre, rocked by the noise, could not understand what they were firing at. There were no standing buildings anymore, and everyone inside was dead. She examined the cannons and saw the new, low angle, and it dawned on her: the cannons were not aiming for buildings this time—but for the canal. The cannonballs suddenly impacted, shattering the stone walls of the canals. The walls exploded, and water gushed onto the city streets.

Dierdre finally understood. They were flooding the tunnels beneath the city.

"NO!" she shrieked.

Dierdre rushed forward, thinking of those they had saved below, desperate to help them before they drowned.

But it was too late. One at a time the canal walls collapsed, sending millions of tons of water rushing belowground. One by one, each tunnel was flooded, and Dierdre could do nothing as she heard below the shrieks of the people she had saved. She watched it all unfold in despair, never feeling so helpless as she watched and heard all those people drown beneath her.

Marco swam up beside her.

"We must save them!" Dierdre cried out.

143

She threw caution to the wind and rushed for one of the openings—but he grabbed her arm.

"It's too late!" he cried. "They're already dead. We must run. Now!"

"NO!" she cried.

She threw off his arm and ran for the iron hatches. She knelt down before one and somehow managed to pry it open.

As she did, water shot up, gushing all over her. There floated up a dead body, one of the people she had saved, a girl, eyes open wide, lifeless. It floated out onto the streets, face up, staring at her, dead.

Suddenly, the city fell silent. All the cannon fire stopped, and Dierdre was even more puzzled to see the ships retreating, going farther out into the harbor, as if leaving the city. All the soldiers were leaving the streets, too, retreating to the harbor, to the ships. Could it be? she wondered. Was the invasion over?

Then something more ominous happened. In the silence, Dierdre watched as all the cannons were adjusted again, turned sideways, this time, to the supporting walls of the harbor. It made no sense. Why would they turn the cannons that way?

Just as it began to dawn on her, with horror, there came a final volley of cannon fire, louder than all the others combined.

And after that, everything changed.

The massive stone walls, ten feet thick, protecting the city from the sea, all exploded into pieces. As they did, the entire weight of the ocean, all of the Sea of Sorrow, came gushing into the Ur. Before her there unfolded the biggest tidal wave she had ever seen.

It was like watching a nightmare unfold before her. The massive wave of water gushed right for them, gaining speed, submerging each block of the city as it went. Within moments, this once-great city was completely underwater.

There was no time for Dierdre to react, to do anything, except to cling to Marco. He clung to her, too, watching in panic as his death approached, both of them too shocked to even scream as the tidal wave came right for them.

And then, a moment later, Dierdre found herself hundreds of feet underwater, tumbling, unable to breathe, hopelessly lost, drowning amidst a city   that   no   longer   was.

CHAPTER THIRTY SIX

Kyra knelt before her mother, feeling a chill as she dwelled on her final word.

Marda.

A journey alone, into the heart of darkness.

And yet as her mother said it, Kyra knew immediately that that was where she was meant to be. Kyra, eyes closed, dwelled on the image, saw flashing before her a land of ash and fire. A land of blackness, of evil. A land of a monster troll race, of grotesque beings that tore people to pieces for fun. A land from which no one returned.

Yet that was, she sensed, where she was needed most, to retrieve the Staff of Truth. And she herself, Kyra knew, was the only one who could do it.

As Kyra dwelled on how to reach Marda, there flashed through her mind the image of a dragon. She was confused as she saw it was not Theos, but another dragon. A baby dragon. And then, suddenly, she knew: it was Theos's son. He was still alive, but barely.

She felt his power coursing through her veins as if it were her own, and for a moment, they were connected. She willed the baby dragon to live. To come back to life. For her. For their shared mission.

Kyra, eyes still closed, raised a palm high into the air, and at that moment she felt herself tapping her power, creating, summoning. An energy burned through her veins and she felt herself no longer at the whim of the universe—but controlling it.

Kyra opened her eyes, and she felt as if she were opening the eyes of the dragon. And at that moment, she knew he would live. And he would listen.

Kyra opened her eyes, burning with questions for her mother, needing to know more. She had a lifetime of questions she wanted answered, most of all: would her mother come with her?

Yet as Kyra opened her eyes, she was aghast to see her mother was gone.

She turned and looked everywhere, and yet she was nowhere to be found. She saw only the ruins of this city, the Lost Temple, heard only the wind howling through this abandoned place, and she could only wonder if she had ever seen her at all.

"MOTHER!"

Yet somehow, she still felt her mother's presence with her, more strongly now than ever. Would her mother come back to her?

Kyra heard something, and she looked to the skies and knew it was the screech of a baby dragon. It filled the air, and as she looked up, she saw

Theos's baby appear. He swooped down from the clouds, diving, screeching, flapping his wings, and she could feel his strength. Though he was a baby, she could already sense his power. She felt a connection with him, a connection even stronger than that she'd had with his father, and she knew they would never be apart. This dragon was filled with rage, filled with a power as wide as the universe.

The baby dove down and finally landed at Kyra's feet, sitting there on the rock, but feet away from her. It flapped its wings, steam emitting from its nostrils, as it stared right at her with its intense, scarlet eyes.

She stepped forward and ran a hand across its scales, down its neck, and she felt its power, like a jolt through her palms.

Theon.

"Theon is your name," she said, feeling it.

Theon raised his head and screeched, as if in approval.

Kyra, in one quick motion, mounted the dragon, climbing onto his back.

"GO FORTH, THEON!" she cried.

Without a moment's hesitation Theon took off, lifting into the air, flapping his great wings. Kyra felt the exhilarating rush of being in the sky, ready to quest anywhere in the world. She looked down as they flew and saw the Lost Temple getting smaller, the ocean waves spread out below, crashing into it, already seeming so minuscule, so far away.

Kyra clutched Theon's fledgling scales as they flew, feeling more powerful than ever, as the world rushed by her with dizzying speed. She could feel the invincible power of the dragon beneath her, lending her strength. It flew high and dove down, roaring, like a caged beast thrilled to be free, thrilled to be reunited with her. It was as if they had known each other forever.

Its great wings flapped furiously, a fraction of the size of his father's; yet Kyra could feel that what Theon lacked in size, he made up for in will. He was, she could sense, a ball of pride and rage. As they flew, Kyra felt as if she were holding onto his father, felt the same bloodline coursing through.

Theon soared higher into a patch of clouds, stretching his wings to full capacity, gliding. She felt he was growing bigger, stronger, with every flap, his wings expanding before her eyes, now a good twenty feet long. His claws expanded and contracted, and he flew faster, she realized, than his father. It took Kyra's breath away.

They finally burst through a patch of clouds, and Kyra looked ahead to the horizon, focusing, knowing where they needed to go. Marda. It summoned her, like some dark corner of her soul urging her to go forth. It was a journey from which she knew there would likely be no return. But that was, she knew, the essence of valor. Her father would never shy from such a journey. And neither would she.

It pained her, the thought of leaving Escalon, leaving her homeland in its time of need; what pained her even more was the idea of leaving her father, especially at the time she was needed most. But that was what her duty demanded of her.

Kyra looked down as they flew, seeing nothing but cloud cover. She felt a burning desire to lay eyes on her homeland before she left it for the last time.

"Down, Theon!" she cried.

Theon hesitated, as if not wishing to, as if knowing her command could have dire consequences. And yet, finally, as she laid a hand on his neck, he obliged.

Theon dipped beneath the clouds, and Kyra felt her heart ache as she saw the countryside beneath her. There was her homeland, sprawled out in all its glory, endless hills of green. They dipped and soared, passing small farming villages, smoke rising from chimneys. They flew over snow-filled plains, over mountains and peaks. They flew over lakes and rivers, waterfalls and plains, the terrain ever-changing. It was the Escalon she loved and knew.

They flew even further, over forts, strongholds, and her heart sank to find many of them smoldering, either abandoned or destroyed. She saw sporadic flames throughout the countryside, and she gasped as she saw the damage that the Pandesians and trolls had inflicted upon her land. It was like a plague had descended upon it. Like the hand of God. Her land, once so bountiful, now looked doomed, cursed.

What made her feel worse was that she felt it was all because of her. If she'd never had that encounter with those soldiers that snowy night, had never discovered a wounded Theos, perhaps none of this would have ever happened. She had been the catalyst, she felt, had been the spark for the revolution of their homeland.

All for what? she wondered. Escalon was now torn to pieces, worse off than it ever was, and her father sat in a dungeon cell. Was this the revolution they were supposed to have? Would it have been better to sit quietly in their towns and not rebel?

She looked down and saw bands of Pandesian troops, marching in perfect columns in their gleaming yellow and blue armor, dragging shackled prisoners, men she recognized immediately by their arms as her father's men. It pained her. She wanted to dip down, to battle the Pandesians right now. Yet she remembered her sacred mission, and she knew she could not afford to deviate.

Kyra looked up ahead and saw on the horizon the dim outline of the capital city of Andros. She knew her father lay in there somewhere, and the

147

thought of it killed her. She could not turn back for him, she knew. Her duty must be to Escalon first.

Yet as she flew past it, seeing the city outlined below, it burned in her veins. She knew she had a duty to fulfill; yet how could she turn her back on her father, her flesh and blood? She was stronger now. She had her powers. She had Theon beneath her. Nothing could stop her this time. This time, she was sure, would be different.

As Kyra flew over the city, she felt herself tingling. She knew she was faced with the decision of a lifetime. And, slowly, the passion of her heart overwhelmed her.

"Turn, Theon," she commanded, her voice steely and cool.

Theon roared, as if in protest, as if he knew nothing good could come of it.

Yet she pulled at his neck, again and again.

"I command you!" she cried, locked in her first power struggle with him.

Kyra closed her eyes and summoned her power and she felt a strength rise within her, a strength that was stronger even than the dragon's, a power that forced him to slowly but surely turn back around.

Theon flew reluctantly, as if in protest. And yet he flew.

Deep down, Kyra knew this was wrong; it was not what she was supposed to be doing. Yet she had no choice. It was what her heart commanded she do. She saw Andros below, and her heart slammed. She would save her father this time. And then she could journey to Marda.

Kyra spotted columns of Pandesian soldiers below, leaned over, and commanded Theon.

"Attack!"

Theon dove, filled with rage himself, not needing to be asked twice. He opened his mouth, roared an earth-shattering roar, and let out as strong a flame as she'd ever seen. Within moments, hundreds of Pandesians, looking up and searching the skies, were aflame, shrieking, burning to their deaths, trapped in their armor.

Theon seemed to take great satisfaction as he flew low to the ground, zigzagging, burning the entire battalion of Pandesian troops. Kyra felt the satisfaction, too. She felt invincible.

Those who remained fled in every direction, running like ants. More battalions of Pandesian soldiers arrived, though, as they neared the city gates, and these were armed, prepared. They looked up and threw spears, fired arrows, taking aim at Theon and Kyra. A wall of death rose up—yet Theon, fearless, refused to rise, to dodge. He stayed low to the ground and faced them head on.

He opened his mouth and breathed down and he burned the first wave of arrows and spears.

148

And then another.

And another.

They all disintegrated and fell back to the ground in a pile of ashes.

Catapults were rolled out, and Kyra gasped as a massive boulder was fired up through the air. Theon breathed fire on it, and yet still it flew, soaring right by her head. Fire could not burn stone, and she knew they were in trouble. And down below, they were rolling out more of them.

Kyra closed her eyes and summoned her power, knowing Theon needed help. She held out a hand, palm forward, and sent out a blast of energy.

As she did, she opened her eyes to see the boulders racing up for them suddenly turn and descend back to the ground. Down below, hundreds of soldiers shrieked as they were flattened, as if comets were falling from the sky.

Theon roared his approval, and Kyra felt good, feeling her own power matching that of the dragon's. She knew that nothing could stop her this time. She would free the capital, and free her father.

They dove lower, closing in on the capital, Theon unleashing a wave of fire and destruction, nothing able to hold them back. Block by block they were taking back the city.

They were just about to reach the dungeons, when suddenly, a sound arose that made the hair rise on her neck, a sound that seemed to tear apart the very heavens. It was so loud, so disorienting, Kyra couldn't even tell where it was coming from. It was louder than a thousand horns, so loud that it sent a wave of energy her way, forcing Theon to fly sideways in the air until he could straighten out again.

Kyra turned and searched the skies, wondering what it could be—and she saw, breaking through the clouds, a sight that seared itself on her soul, a sight that she would never forget. It was the most terrifying sight of her life.

There appeared, inexplicably, the face of a dragon, emerging from the clouds. It was a roaring, enormous dragon, ten times the size of Theon. Bigger even than Theos.

Then, behind it, there appeared another dragon.

And another.

An army of dragons burst through the clouds, shrieking, blackening the sky. They breathed a wall of fire as they roared, all reaching out with their claws—and all flying right for Theon.

They came too fast, too unexpected, and there was no time to react.

And then, a moment later, Kyra felt Theon lurch. She looked back and saw one of the dragons had closed in from behind, had reached out with its claw and grabbed Theon's tail. He spun Theon around in the air with his great might, and then threw him.

Theon was spinning out of control through the sky, Kyra on his back, the world a blur of motion all around her as she tried her best to hang on. They spun again and again, the spinning never ending, and soon they were plunging straight down toward the ground. Nothing could stop their fall.

Kyra looked down and saw a battalion of Pandesian soldiers below awaiting her. She then looked back up to the sky, and the last thing she saw before she hit the ground was the army of dragons, descending from the sky, claws out, and coming right for her.

Coming soon!

Book #5 in KINGS AND SORCERERS

Books by Morgan Rice

KINGS AND SORCERERS
RISE OF THE DRAGONS
RISE OF THE VALIANT
THE WEIGHT OF HONOR
A FORGE OF VALOR

THE SORCERER'S RING
A QUEST OF HEROES
A MARCH OF KINGS
A FATE OF DRAGONS
A CRY OF HONOR
A VOW OF GLORY
A CHARGE OF VALOR
A RITE OF SWORDS
A GRANT OF ARMS
A SKY OF SPELLS
A SEA OF SHIELDS
A REIGN OF STEEL
A LAND OF FIRE
A RULE OF QUEENS
AN OATH OF BROTHERS
A DREAM OF MORTALS

THE SURVIVAL TRILOGY
ARENA ONE (Book #1)
ARENA TWO (Book #2)

the Vampire Journals
turned (book #1)
loved (book #2)
betrayed (book #3)
destined (book #4)
desired (book #5)
betrothed (book #6)
vowed (book #7)
found (book #8)
resurrected (book #9)
craved (book #10)
fated (book #11)

About Morgan Rice

Morgan Rice is the #1 bestselling and USA Today bestselling author of the epic fantasy series THE SORCERER'S RING, comprising seventeen books; of the #1 bestselling series THE VAMPIRE JOURNALS, comprising eleven books (and counting); of the #1 bestselling series THE SURVIVAL TRILOGY, a post-apocalyptic thriller comprising two books (and counting); and of the new epic fantasy series KINGS AND SORCERERS. Morgan's books are available in audio and print editions, and translations are available in over 25 languages.

Morgan loves to hear from you, so please feel free to visit www.morganricebooks.com to join the email list, receive a free book, receive free giveaways, download the free app, get the latest exclusive news, connect on Facebook and Twitter, and stay in touch!

CPSIA information can be obtained
at www.ICGtesting.com
Printed in the USA
BVOW03s0807281216
472029BV00008B/85/P